THE JOSHUA ABOMINATION

MARK AKST

Printed in the United States of America
Hardcover ISBN: 979-8-9995108-0-8
Paperback ISBN: 979-8-9995108-1-5
Ebook ISBN: 979-8-9995108-2-2

Mark Akst
Ft. Lauderdale FL
markakst.com

TABLE OF CONTENTS

THE SILVER TRUMPET

The late summer of 73 CE—In the dying City of Jerusalem, just as the Roman Army under General Titus breached its North wall after a three year bloody siege, choking clouds of black smoke swirled around everything, burning the survivor's eyes and making it almost impossible to see. The Romans were torching everything! The only sound above the hysterical screams of the Jewish inhabitants running from the advancing Roman soldiers for fear of death, rape or enslavement was the constant thuds of huge stone balls hurled by Roman catapults against the crumbling massive city walls. A portion of the North wall had fallen, creating an opening into which the Roman legions poured.

Aaron ben Halevi, an eight year old Jewish boy, small for his age and now half-starved, slinked around the city's underground water and sewer tunnels like a cat, stealing food and water from the four major Jewish factions who had, until now, controlled different parts of the city. In the four months since he had been abruptly forced to live in the underground tunnels and sewers to save his life, he had grown so familiar with the underground system that he could almost navigate it blindfolded. Regardless of his young age, he was a born survivor with razor-sharp instincts; a fact that let him eat better than most—at least better than the hundreds of bone-thin corpses, dead from starvation and thrown over the walls daily by the city's defenders to keep the rancid smell of death in the city at tolerable levels and to annoy the surrounding Roman army encircling the city with the stench. The problem was that there were fewer and fewer Jewish defenders to throw the dead from the massive stone walls that protected the city.

The four Jewish factions—monarchists, zealots, populists, and the High Priests—controlled different sections of the city and hated each other more than the invading Romans. In truth, according to Jewish historian Flavius Josephus, infighting between these Jewish factions killed more Jewish defenders than the Romans did. Only in the last days before the city fell did the four Jewish factions realize their mistake and unite against Rome. But it was too late to save themselves and the Holy City from complete capitulation and destruction. It was a major strategic error which future generations of Jews would vow never to repeat.

Moreover, little Aaron, nicknamed Ari by his father, had not yet realized the extreme life threatening danger he was in by crawling through the water tunnels and sewers to steal food from each faction. By being almost oblivious to the mortal dangers surrounding him, he had become fearless, which helped him survive. If he had been caught, the various Jewish factions would have put him to death as quickly as the Romans, especially since he was from a family of Temple priests who many blamed for their present calamity. The only good news about living in the city's underground tunnels and sewers was that the black smoke from the fires which burned his eyes and lungs above ground rarely penetrated so deep under the city. Also, the sound of the monstrously big Roman stone balls being hurled against the city's outer walls making the ground tremble was greatly muffled at this depth. The bad news was that the fires, smoke, and incessant pounding of catapulted stone balls against the outer walls had increased so much that there was no longer a reprieve from the terror.

Was it little Ari's survival instinct or just dumb luck allowing him to make the underground of the city his own? Actually, to Ari, his survival or death never entered his mind. Because of his young age, he didn't realize that he was dangerously thin from lack of proper food or that his daily hunts for sustenance were a matter of life or death. Traveling around the city underground to steal food was all a big game to this eight year old boy. Without consciously thinking about it, there was something deep inside him, guiding him and making him fearless.

In truth, there was a part of him that deeply enjoyed his new freedom of movement away from his now dead parents. His parents had been very strict raising him. They were training him to take his place as a hereditary Temple priest. This required long hours of study of the Jewish Holy books. Indeed, he could already speak, read and write Hebrew, the language of the Bible; Aramaic, the common tongue of the Middle East of that era; and Greek, the common tongue of the Roman conquerors. These academic accomplishments, however, came at the cost of his freedom. No play time for him. Nevertheless, he deeply loved his parents and keenly missed them. But he also dearly loved his newfound freedom of movement around the city. He had never stepped foot on the Temple Mount, as he was still too young to partake in the religious ceremonies taking place there. Currently, it was the only place in Jerusalem he had not visited. He had even managed to walk around King Herod's palace, visiting in the early morning hours when all the defenders were asleep to steal the best of their meager food supply.

He was raised in the priestly quarter of the city close to the Temple Mount. His parent's house was relatively big for houses inside the city, so he had his own bedroom to himself.

He did not have any brothers or sisters. Because of his family's priestly status, he did not have any playmates or toys either—just studying and more studying. His father was one of two priests whose family descended from generations chosen to blow one of the two Holy Silver Trumpets on Jewish holidays. The trumpets were blown from the corners of the Temple Mount and called the Jewish people to prayer. On major Jewish holidays, there would be hundreds of thousands of Jews listening to the trumpets summoning them as they made their way to the Temple Mount to pray.

Although too young to be allowed on the Temple Mount, he had heard and seen his father from the street below, blowing the silver trumpet from the marble cornerstone high above the city. The height of the corner of the Temple Mount wall where his father stood was shockingly high to a small boy. Indeed, to anyone, because it was more than one hundred and five feet (33m) above street level, overlooking all of Jerusalem.

It had been about four months since his parents had been murdered. He guessed that it was men from one of the Jewish factions that had come into their house and ransacked it looking for food and valuables. He distinctly remembered his father picking him up and dropping him into a small private well in the back of their house to avoid being killed. The last thing his father said to him was "Hold your breath and look for the tunnel out!" With that, he let go, plunging Ari into the cool well water almost 20 feet (6.1m) beneath the surface—saving his life. Ari had never learned to swim, so he never forgot the terror he felt when his whole body submerged beneath the dark well water. But as he popped up gasping for air, his hand desperately grasped onto a nook in the rock wall allowing him to cling to a side of the well, get his senses back, and take stock of his new predicament. From there he felt his way to an opening in the wall just big enough for him to squeeze through and escape, thus entering the city's extensive and bewildering underground tunnel system. He never saw his parents again. All he heard was the muffled sounds of a fight. Since then, he had been back to his house several times looking for them—hoping to meet them there if they were still alive—leaving them small handwritten notes that he was still alive and to meet him there or leave a note for him. Every time he returned, he experienced the crushing loneliness of being ripped from them and his home. He didn't like thinking about it, so he forced himself not to dwell on it. Moreover, after his third return visit to his former home, he became convinced that his parents were murdered, and that their bodies were probably tossed over the wall with the other dead. Luckily, though, on his first return visit to his home, he remembered where his father had hidden a cache of oil lamps with a supply of olive oil, flints, and enough linen to use for a fuse. He had since distributed all these lamps at critical points in the underground water tunnel system to give him light when he needed it, which made it possible for him to travel to the farthest corners of the city without getting lost.

When he looked down from the city walls last night, he saw the encircling Roman legions at the base of the wall and heard the adults on the street hysterically talking about how the Roman soldiers had just breached the northern wall of the city. He overheard that they had overrun the last ditch defenses, creating carnage everywhere, walking over dead bodies to kill more and more people as they advanced. He instinctively knew his life was about to change. He also knew that he could leave the city anytime he wanted. He had followed several water tunnels outside the city under the Roman legion encampments and beyond but had always decided to return.

However, there was one thing that kept looming larger and larger on his mind. He was so curious about how the Holy Temple looked. He had not dared to go because his father had forbidden him. But before he left the city, he just wanted to see it—just once. The Roman army was quickly overrunning the city. What made up his mind was when he climbed out of a street gutter opening, looked up and saw smoke billowing from the Temple Mount. He knew he had to visit the Holy Temple now or never. Luckily there were still sections of the underground water and sewer tunnels where there was no smoke and thus were still breathable. Because of his youth, Ari still didn't fully comprehend his own mortal danger or the serious state of the collapse of Jerusalem.

A while ago he had discovered where one of the sewer tunnels split into two, below where he guessed the Temple was located. One of the tunnels went up at a forty five degree angle and smelled particularly fowl. By now Ari was very familiar with the smell of dead human bodies. But this particular tunnel smelled different—he guessed that it was the stench of dead animal bodies sacrificed on the Temple Altar that his father had described. Ari guessed that this was the runoff tunnel connected to the drainage channel that cut into the Temple Altar, which would lead to the top of the Temple Mount. Indeed, if he remembered his father's description correctly, this shaft would lead to the stone altar located in the inner courtyard, very close to the front of the Temple itself. Even though this new tunnel—more like a shaft really, going up at a steep angle—was somewhat small, Ari still knew he could squeeze through. He had no fear of getting stuck. In fact, getting stuck in it never occurred to him— due to the audacity and stupidity of youth!

As he started his climb to the top of the Temple Mount in this new tunnel, Ari could hardly breathe due to the stench of dead animal parts and dried blood that surrounded him. Even his body brushing against the walls of this tunnel disgusted him. Ari was lucky that it had not rained recently, so the blood and animal entrails had dried making the tunnel surface sticky and giving him firm footing to make his climb possible. Rain would have cleared the drainage channel but also made it too slippery to climb. Curiosity and determination drove him on.

When he finally reached the top and climbed out of the drainage shaft alongside the Altar of Burnt Offerings on the Temple Mount, what he saw surprised him. The place was empty and silent except for the crackling of fire and smell of burning wood as the roof of the surrounding colonnade burned. He had just missed the four sentries that the Roman General Titus had placed there to guard the inner Temple. Even though the General had given strict orders to guard it—permitting no one to enter before he arrived—these orders had been countermanded by the Roman Centurion trying to control the blaze of the raging fire next door. The fact that the fire was approaching the Temple treasure storerooms and the distinct possibility of more loot hastened the Roman guards departure.

Standing there, getting his bearings, Ari also noticed that the huge bronze doors to the Temple were wide open. He remembered that according to his father, these doors should always remain closed except on specific Jewish Holy Days. Without a further thought on the matter, Ari sprinted to see what lay inside—hoping to see for himself where God lives! It was getting dark and the smoke from the surrounding fire was getting much more noticeable. He knew he did not have much time before someone saw him, so he quickly entered the Temple and climbed the twelve steps leading to the entrance. The sun was beaming through the immense wide open doors at his back, lighting the path ahead. What first caught his eye was the huge Altar of Incense at the back of the room. Then, his eyes fell on the even larger golden Temple Menorah to his left which reached 12 feet (3.6m) tall, and the shiny solid silver Table of Showbread to his right. He even dared to part the curtain behind the Altar of Incense and peek into the inner sanctum of the Holy of Holies, where the Ark of the Covenant was supposed to reside. But the sunlight did not penetrate to that area, and the utter blackness frightened him enough to withdraw and immediately turn to leave.

What caught his eye now were the two shiny solid silver trumpets, both almost six feet (1.8m) long, lying in a crossed position on top of the silver table. They glowed brightly from the sunlight, drawing the little boy to it. He remembered that he had heard his father blow one. The sight of the trumpets thrilled him—not because of any religious reason, but because in them he saw a toy—a plaything. What eight year old boy doesn't want a horn to blow? And he had never had a toy. As he gently lifted up one of the silver trumpets and held it, he knew this was his. While he couldn't wait to blow it, he also knew that he needed to quickly escape with his new toy. He had no idea that as the direct descendent of Aaron, brother to Moses and High Priest of the Temple by God's law, he was the only one permitted to touch the Holy Trumpet (the Biblical name for a horn). This trumpet that was sounded to summon millions of Jews to pray at the Holy Temple; this trumpet that High Priests sounded while walking in front of the Jewish multitudes as they returned to Israel from their Babylonian Exile; this trumpet that was sounded a thousand years prior to call the Hebrew tribes to war in God's name. The call was answered by the sound of the ram's horn—called the Shofar—blown from the mountain tops across Judea, Samaria and the Galilee. Thus, this Holy Trumpet was also a weapon of unearthly power that could call the Lord God Himself to Holy War if wielded by a hereditary High Priest in times of trouble. But for little Ari, all he knew was that he had a shiny new toy. For him, that was that.

He moved quickly now carrying the trumpet. It was solid silver and getting a little heavy for him. But he was determined to take it, even if he had to drag it behind him. However, as he was approaching the Temple entrance, he stopped cold. Something surprised him. When he had entered the Temple he was looking up and forward. But now, looking down at the floor, he saw the fallen body of a High Priest. Ari had seen enough dead bodies recently to know one when he saw one, which at this point didn't bother him at all. In fact, the condition of this man's body told him that his death was recent. Moreover, this body was dressed in blue robes like his father wore, so he knew immediately that the man was a High Priest. The position of the body also told Ari that the priest had tried to stop someone from entering when he was killed and tossed aside.

Additionally, Ari was familiar with the High Priest's robe since he had seen his father wear one similar, and his father always had food or candy in two secret pockets hidden in its folds. So Ari stopped for a second, put down his trumpet and started to search the robes of the dead man. While searching, he started to speak to the dead priest as if he was alive, saying, "I apologize for going into your pocket. I hope you don't mind but I'm hungry and am just looking for some food or candy." Sure enough, in the first pocket he found a leather pouch with sweet cakes—the same his father had always given him. He thought, *What luck! Food!* He now quickened his search, looking for the second hidden pocket in the robe. Pulling back a few more folds in the blue cloth of the robe, his fingers found the second pocket and grabbed a leather pouch, pulling it out. He quickly untied the knot holding it closed and looked inside. To his amazement, he saw at least a dozen gold coins—a fortune! But he didn't have time to count it. So he hurriedly grabbed both pouches and walked quickly, almost running, dragging his silver horn behind him to the drainage hole next to the altar. He and his horn quickly disappeared into the hole. Feeling safe, he then stopped to take a break and eat his newfound sweet cakes. He was famished. His luck still held, for just as he was swallowing the last of his food, he could hear Roman soldiers entering the Inner Courtyard of the Temple and heading straight for its entrance. They missed him by minutes!

Ari took a chance and popped his head above the surface of the drainage hole, just enough so he was able to see the Romans. It was an entire company of Roman soldiers. In front of this company of soldiers was a man dressed in a shiny gold breast plate, shiny gold helmet with red feathers sprouting from its top, and a flowing red cape covering his shoulders down to his boots. Ari had never seen such a luxurious uniform. He didn't know it, but he was looking at the Roman General Titus—in charge of the siege and now the sack of Jerusalem.

General Titus immediately entered the Temple surrounded by his men to survey his conquest and see where the Jewish God lived. Ari knew that the non-Jewish pagan Romans entering the Temple were committing sacrilege. But he also knew the situation was well beyond that now. He thought to himself, *God would not approve.* Ari could also hear the commotion of loud soldier voices outside the Inner Courtyard walls. But whether they were trying to put out existing fires or starting new ones, Ari couldn't tell.

General Titus was not inside the Temple long before he realized that the fire on the colonnade roof next to the Temple was out of control and would soon consume everything. As he was a methodical man, he had been well briefed by his Jewish advisors and indeed his Jewish princess and mistress, Berenice, granddaughter to Herod the Great, as to what objects he would find inside. He immediately gave orders to his soldiers to remove everything as quickly and as gently as possible before the building collapsed. As his soldiers were removing the Holy objects from the Temple, he realized that one of the silver trumpets was missing. There were supposed to be two! He knew that this was a massive security failure. He would be very embarrassed to share this with his father, Vespasian, who left him in charge of successfully completing the conquest and subjugation of Judea. His father was now marching on Rome with 24 legions, supporting him to be proclaimed the next Caesar. Herod Agrippa, brother to Titus' mistress Berenice, was concurrently bribing Roman Senators with Jewish gold to make sure Vespasian was confirmed by the Senate as Caesar upon his arrival. They were leaving nothing to chance. Moreover, Titus knew what extraordinary value his Jewish allies placed on these Temple objects. And now a Holy Trumpet was missing! How embarrassing in front of his allies! It was the greatest paradox of this conquest that while he was sacking Judea and Jerusalem, Jews were making sure his family came to power in Rome.

Ordinarily, he would start executing his soldiers until he found the one or ones who stole it. But if he started disciplining his men in the middle of sacking and raping the city they very well could turn on him. His soldiers considered the sack of the city extra payment for such a long, hard war. So he made a split second decision not to say anything—to pretend all the Holy Jewish items were found in place and accounted for. To this day, his triumphal arch in Rome includes sculpted images of two trumpets alongside other looted items from the temple.

He did, however, make a silent promise to himself to crucify the guilty person or persons who took that trumpet if he ever found them.

Of course, little Ari knew nothing of the political problems troubling General Titus, and quite frankly, he didn't care. All he knew was that the smoke was getting too thick and starting to burn his throat and lungs as he inhaled. Also, he could now feel the heat from the encroaching fire. His survival instinct told him it was time to leave. So down he went along the shaft, dragging his prized toy behind him with one hand and an oil lamp in the other to light the way. He also cleverly tied the leather pouch containing the gold coins to his wrist, freeing his hands. His one miscalculation, however, was that he forgot about the tight turn in the tunnel below street level. His toy horn was too long and stiff to make the turn. In fact, it got stuck when he tried to pull it through. No matter how he tried, he could not budge it— his pulling and pushing only stuck it more firmly in place.

He was disappointed. But before leaving it behind, he decided that he would put his lips on the mouthpiece and try to blow it just once to hear how it sounded. Unfortunately, not only had his father not yet trained him on the way to use his lips and control his breath to blow a trumpet, but he was still too winded and tired from his trip to the top of the Temple Mount. Nope—not even a small toot sounded from his toy. Frustrated, he left it there, buried under almost eighty feet (24m) of rock but just above the sludge line of the drainage shaft. Over the centuries, the top of the Temple Mount was destroyed and rebuilt many times—each a bloody destruction. First came the Romans (twice destroying it), then Byzantines, then Arabs, Persians, Crusaders, then the Arabs again, Mamluks, and finally the Turkish Ottomans. Each had their own religious agenda for the Holy Temple Mount. Over the centuries, safely below all this, the once brilliantly shiny silver trumpet became deeply tarnished to a blackish brown color, further hiding it by camouflaging against the surrounding ancient rock. Was it lost forever, or were the rocks and little Ari's audacious theft protecting it? Was it just waiting to be discovered and sounded again over a Jewish Jerusalem? For isn't it true that God sometimes works in strange ways?

As for little Ari, he could smell the black smoke of the burning city permeating down to where he was below street level. He was keenly aware that his newfound gold coins would help him to somehow survive outside the walls of Jerusalem. He also knew exactly the underground tunnel that would lead him outside the city beyond the Roman military lines. So he took a breath and bravely decided this was the moment for him to leave his home—the only place he ever knew—to save himself.

Crouching most of the time to avoid hitting his head, he traveled quickly through Jerusalem's underground tunnel system. He emptied two oil lamps on the way through those dark, dank tunnels before he could see the daylight from an opening, now miles beyond the city walls. As he emerged into the light and greenery of the surrounding landscape he was pleasantly surprised how fresh the air smelled. It was the first time in months that he didn't smell the rancid stench of dead rotting flesh or the stinging smell of black smoke burning his nostrils. Also, he noticed how quiet the area was. No more pounding of Roman catapult stone balls against the hard city stone walls or the never ending screams and cries of the wounded. It only took him a moment to take a breath and feel mentally refreshed by his new surroundings. In the distance he noticed a group of men laughing while sitting near a pool of clear water with the sound of a gurgling stream running into it. Ari thought to himself, *This is so different from where I just came from.* He also noticed more than a dozen camels with their heads bent low, guzzling water from the pool. He guessed that this must be a trading caravan which he had heard about. Indeed, he had heard about camels too but had never seen one.

As he approached the group of men sitting by the water, a huge man with a well-kept, full gray beard stood up to greet him. He wore a flowing white robe and white turban, with part of the turban linen falling to one side to reveal a sunburnt and deeply lined face from decades in the desert sun. His tightly bound waist band held a huge curved scimitar sword.

Ari gathered his strength and greeted him in Aramaic, not Hebrew, formally introducing himself as Aaron ben Halevi, since he guessed that the big man must be the leader and not Jewish. Ari's instinct proved correct. Sheikh Ibn al Khalid was not only the caravan owner but King of the Nabateans—the Arab tribe which controlled all the trading routes between the Roman Empire and Asia. And King Ibn al Khalid was truly shocked by what he saw standing in front of him. He asked himself, "Am I looking at a human or a small creature?" Surprisingly, the creature spoke perfect Aramaic to him and now held out a gold coin, asking for passage on his caravan. But this creature was completely covered in black soot and smelled of feces and death. Its ragged clothes barely covered its body, contrasting sharply with the extreme value of the gold coin held in its raised little hand. But the King was not stupid. He looked above and beyond the boy's head to see black smoke rising miles into the sky from the dying city and knew Ari was one of the Jews fleeing and desperate to survive. He admired the boy's courage and instantly felt a strong fatherly sense of protection towards the brave, little fellow since he missed his own children who were hundreds of miles away. Moreover, this hard boiled, shrewd desert chieftain did not believe in luck or coincidence but instinctively sensed that the only way this little boy could have survived the terrible destruction of the city and been guided to him amidst the chaos of the surrounding war was if God walked with the boy. The desert people call it Barakah. It literally means blessing, referring to the spiritual power of God that flows to special people. Thus, these special people are deeply respected and treated almost like prophets amongst the desert tribes. So, when he heard little Ari speak, it surprised King Ibn al Khalid that the Barakah was so strong with the boy regardless of his young age.

All Ari knew was that his luck held when the King said, "Put your money away. You are my guest. Maybe later when you have regained your strength you can work for me if you want. I will teach you how to ride a camel and the ways of the desert. Here, drink as much as you want." As he offered a calf skin water bag to Ari, almost as big as Ari himself, he said, "Our camels have finished drinking. Bathe yourself in the pool while I find you some new clothes. And after washing join us for some roast lamb, bread and hummus."

While washing himself, one of the men laughed as he yelled to Ari, "Let us all pray to God that the Roman soldiers come here to drink. You are so dirty you have poisoned the water for a week!"

Ari realized these men hated the Romans as much as he did. So he also laughed, yelling back, "By the way, where are we going?"

The camel driver replied, "We are merchants trading our goods, with our saddle bags full of Judean royal blue and purple dye powders which are more valuable than gold; trading it first in Mesopotamia, then Persia, then India, then back to Babylon." That response thrilled Ari to the bone, for he had never been anywhere outside of Jerusalem and was about to see more of the world than most people of the time. He also knew he had found a home among these hospitable desert tribesmen.

Decades later, because of the deep respect the desert tribes held for him and his sharp business sense, Ari was able to develop the largest caravan trading network in the Middle East. There was even a rumor in Babylon amongst his fellow Jews that he had married another wife in India who was a princess, the daughter of a Maharajah. Some speculated that the marriage was how he was able to gain control of the largest diamond mine in the world at the time. But this was only a rumor. In his old age, sitting in his big comfortable villa overlooking the fabulous City of Babylon, at the crossroads of the ancient world located on the banks of the Euphrates River in Mesopotamia (modern day Iraq), he possessed wealth beyond counting. He also had considerable political power, as one of ten members of the Persian Empire's governing council reporting directly to the Shah. But what he loved most was telling stories to his many grandchildren about his adventures traveling and, of course, about the fall of his beloved Jerusalem—especially about the time when he entered the Holy of Holies in the Temple itself, and how he had saved and hid—he changed the story over the years from stolen as a toy for himself to "saved"—one of the Holy Silver Temple Trumpets from the Roman defilers. His grandchildren loved their grandfather very much, but also knew he had a tendency to exaggerate when telling stories. They found this shocking story about the Holy Silver Trumpet still under the Temple Mount hard to believe.

There was really only one person who would have believed his story about taking the silver trumpet from the Holy Temple, and that was Caesar himself, the now Roman Emperor Titus. And he would have had Ari crucified on the spot had he heard it. However, he never did hear the story. So, again, did Aaron ben Halevi's luck hold or was it God's plan all along?

The only sad moment in Ari's life came every time he raised his glass of wine at the dinner table during Jewish holidays with the toast "Next year in Jerusalem," a toast Jews give so that they never forget their city. When making that toast, he would always remember the smell of the stinking black smoke in his nostrils and hear the cries of the dying—but only for a moment. Regardless of his success in later life, he never really got over his childhood trauma of losing his parents in a dying city. He never again visited Jerusalem.

Oh yes, there was one more thing old Grandpa Ari loved to do. It was to blow the Shofar—made from a ram's horn—on the Jewish Holidays in the biggest synagogue in Babylon. His fellow congregants would always praise him, saying that he was a natural at it—blowing the horn with such raw power and beauty that even God could hear it. Over the centuries, both Ari and his story about the Holy Silver Trumpet passed into family legend.

CHAPTER TWO

.୶ୡୡ.

LEAVE NO ONE BEHIND!

The highly classified aerial battleship, nicknamed Dragon Fire, fitted with the latest laser weaponry and antigravity fusion engine, was returning to the State of Israel from a dangerous but successful mission. On board was Colonel Eric Jansen, handsome military hero, archeologist and still secret Mossad (Israeli spy agency) operative; Mark Cohn, Eric's older married partner and famous treasure hunter; their good friend Colonel Sam Reichman, the new Chief of Mossad due to the recent political shakeup in the Israeli government; his wife Alisa, also a lethal Mossad operative; and the two pilots Captain Gil Sofer and Lieutenant Elon Dagen. The internal Israeli military coup they just helped prevent and then cover up had guaranteed democracy's future in Israel or so they all hoped.

Before they landed at Hatzor Airbase in central Israel, Eric Jansen received a call on his cell from Jacob Kurtz, outwardly the multi-millionaire owner of the largest public relations, advertising and media company in Israel, but secretly the head of the umbrella intelligence agency in charge of all the country's covert and intelligence operations and strategic military objectives. In other words, the most powerful man in Israel after the Prime Minister. He also happened to be a good friend and neighbor of both Eric and Mark and just announced his engagement to Eric's mother, Miriam Jansen.

Eric recognized Jacob's number, so he answered the call without saying hello. "You don't even let me get off the plane. What's up?"

Jacob replied, "The last time we spoke, I asked you if you wanted to run for prime minister. I still haven't gotten an answer."

Eric quickly said, "Yes. My answer is yes! I plan to be the first openly gay Prime Minister of Israel."

Jacob then said, "I thought you would say that. So I prepared a little homecoming for you when you get off the plane. Make sure you're the first one off."

With that, Jacob curtly hung up the phone, as was his custom. Eric turned to everyone seated and said, "Jacob wants me to be the first one off, if no one minds?" They all didn't care.

The most technologically advanced aerial battleship in the world proceeded to land vertically while the people inside felt no movement at all. This supersonic plane was more spaceship than anything else. When the door opened, the plane was still using its anti-gravity fusion engine to silently float one foot (.3m) above the ground, making for an easy exit.

When six foot two (1.9m) Eric Jansen with movie star good looks appeared at the exit door of the aerial battleship, the uniformed crowd of military soldiers that had gathered to welcome him home burst into applause shouting his name, "Eric" over and over again. They all knew about his past exploits of capturing and killing terrorists and saving a busload of Israeli hostages. To them, he was a true hero.

Since he knew that it was public knowledge that the current prime minister had just resigned under dubious circumstances, he decided to spontaneously test the waters. So Eric raised both hands over his head, showing two fingers in a V shape, and loudly said, "Thank you for your warm welcome. But I need to tell you all something. I have decided to run for Prime Minister of the State of Israel. I think I can help lead our nation to peace, prosperity and security. And I also want to introduce you to my longtime married partner, Mark Cohn." With that, Eric took Mark's hand and held it up along with his. The crowd vigorously applauded them both, now being joined by more and more soldiers from the base. The enthusiastic crowd followed them to their cars.

Sam and Alisa Reichman drove Eric and Mark home. The minute Eric walked in the door of his house, his cellphone rang again. It was Jacob saying, "That went well. I saw the whole thing on video screen taken by one of my people in the crowd."

All Eric said in response was, "Next time, no uniforms, no military. I need to be a civilian PM."

Jacob replied, "Point taken. Tomorrow, be in my office at my house at 3 p.m. for a political strategy campaign meeting. It's important. I need to introduce you to someone, so Mark should come too." Then he hung up.

Mark knew that Eric always needed to release tension by making love after returning from a dangerous government mission or extreme sporting event. It was something in Eric's body movements and eyes that alerted him to his partner's needs. He didn't have to wait long. Mark wasn't privy to the details, but guessed that what must have happened on Eric's recent mountain climbing expedition was very dangerous. So, as soon as Eric got off his phone call, he looked straight into Mark's eyes, and they both knowingly flew into each other's arms, made love, then had dinner at a local restaurant and fell asleep together in their own bed. They slept late the next morning.

Since Jacob's house was just above theirs on the same road near Caesarea, they decided to walk to the meeting. Parked in front of his house was a car they didn't recognize. They correctly assumed that the car belonged to the new person who would be attending the meeting. They both also knew that Jacob's security cameras were monitoring their every step. In fact, as they approached his front door, it automatically opened. While walking through the door, Mark commented, "When the automatic door opens like that before we even knock, it always seems creepy to me."

Eric replied, "It's just the technology working like it should."

Jacob's house was built in the style of a Roman villa with an interior garden courtyard, or peristyle as it is called in Greek. The place was luxurious, fit for any ancient Roman noble. But Eric and Mark had visited many times, and although very impressed at first, they now hardly noticed the expensive inlaid black marble floors and huge wall murals depicting hunting scenes in ancient Judea as they walked through the garden to his office.

Upon entering, they saw Jacob and a stranger sitting chatting. Both immediately stood as Jacob made the introductions. Jacob introduced Boaz Bergman who liked to be called Bo. Bo had dark blond hair that was slightly receding, medium height, and was somewhat overweight. In fact, his appearance was average except for his icy cold blue eyes. His very non-threatening looks belied the most politically astute mind in the country. They all sat and made themselves comfortable as Jacob went on to explain, "I asked you here today to meet Bo. I recommend that you hire him as your political strategist, since you are a political novice and I think Bo is a genius at building new candidate's political careers. He can help you navigate the tricky political scene here. I also briefed him on both of your backgrounds. Let me further say that acting as your political strategist, he will be your combined campaign manager, chief of staff and speech writer." Eric just sat there listening.

The rest of the meeting was for getting to know each other, and they were all trying hard to be charming. During the meeting, Bo said, "To give you a little of my background, I am responsible for the successful careers of one Prime Minister, two Presidents of the Knesset and three current Knesset members. However, I only concentrate on one candidate's career at time. I have also served as a Captain in the Israeli Defense Forces." He continued, looking straight at Eric, "I have only one question for you. Do you want to be Prime Minister?"

Eric strongly replied, looking straight in Bo's eyes, "Yes!" But Bo didn't seem convinced. It was now Eric's turn to ask a question, "Bo, I was wondering how old you are?"

Bo replied, "I am 35 years old. And I know why you asked. I am very proficient on the internet. I grew up with it—all aspects of it—from marketing podcasts to cybersecurity." This answer impressed Eric because it was the exact reason why he asked the question. Eric's instinct told him that he needed someone young enough to have strong internet skills.

Eric made his decision to hire Bo based on this response and said, "Fine, you're hired. But I don't know how much you cost." Bo side-stepped both Eric's response and question by not answering. By Bo's reaction, Eric and Mark realized they were also being interviewed by Bo to see if they were the right fit for him.

For the next hour the conversation continued with light banter amongst the four men as they were trying to get a read on one another. Jacob, in particular, was listening to every body twitch or tone change in the conversation. During that time, Bo displayed a remarkable sense of humor and ability to put everyone at ease. Finally, Eric, in passing, mentioned, "During my entire Special Forces and Mossad military career I have always put my country, Israel, first above all else, even my own life."

Immediately after Eric said this, Bo exclaimed, as if he had just made a decision, "Good. From now on, you're mine. You will go, do, and say only what I tell you. You don't speak to any press people without my permission. And whatever you do, don't accept any political contributions from anyone. Israel has extremely strict laws governing campaign contributions. I mean strict as in you can ruin your career if you don't follow the rules. And you don't know the rules yet. That means all fundraising goes through me. Refer any talk of campaign funding or donations to me. To avoid any problems along those lines you will self-fund my salary. Israeli campaign rules permit a candidate to hire a consultant as a political strategist. The next meeting will be in two days at 11 a.m. It will be at my old campaign office which I still use. Mark, you are also invited. Now I must leave. I will be busy getting ready for the meeting. I will text you the address of your new temporary campaign headquarters." With that, Bo said goodbye and left. After Bo departed, both Eric and Mark quizzically looked at one another. Mark spoke first since he handled all the financial arrangements in their marriage. Eric knew he had made a lot of money from his promotional deals concerning his successful archeological expeditions but really didn't concern himself with finances. He left all that for Mark to manage.

All Mark said was, "Hiring Bo is like ordering off a restaurant menu with no prices next to the items!"

Jacob retorted, "But this is how to kickstart Eric's campaign. In my opinion, he is vital to Eric's campaign success. And I am sure you can afford him."

Eric said nothing but looked at Mark. Mark knew that look. It was the look that Eric had when he gave up control to Mark about money. Mark didn't see it often and he wasn't about to let his partner down. So all Mark said was, "Sure, we'll fund Bo's salary and expenses. I will just have to eat cheese sandwiches from now on." Then he turned to Jacob and said, "I would appreciate a little heads up in the future about major expenses." Jacob didn't reply and had no real sympathy because he knew through the research at his disposal from the Israeli intelligence agencies that Mark was worth more than $50 million. Most of that was in the United States. He also knew that Mark had given specific instructions in his will that Eric was to receive it all upon Mark's death, and that Eric had no idea Mark was worth that much. He also knew that Mark didn't know that he knew this or about his involvement as the director of the entire Israeli intelligence establishment.

So, before anything else could be said, Jacob stood up saying, "Let's go for drinks and dinner on me. I also invited Miriam to join us."

Mark liked Miriam, his mother-in-law, and liked socializing with her. But he wondered if Eric was completely cool with Jacob and his mother's engagement. They had announced their engagement before Eric and Mark's recent trip to the island of Tenerife. And this was the first time they were going to see her since the announcement. Mark turned to Eric and said, "Sure, let's go. It will be fun." But he could tell by Eric's short nod of agreement and half smile that Eric wasn't relaxed about it. Mark thought that Eric would probably be more relaxed facing a squad of terrorists or skydiving rather than dealing with his mother's new relationship.

What Eric couldn't tell Mark was the thing that made him uncomfortable with his mother's relationship with Jacob was that behind his charming, media mogul facade, Jacob was the second most powerful man in the country and a killer like himself. And he was almost sure his mother wasn't aware of this. Just as Mark, after years of marriage to Eric, was only dimly aware of the scope of Eric's past. This was not accidental on Eric's part. Eric needed Mark emotionally to keep the killer part of him, or as Mark called it, his black side, out of sight and under control and himself in balance. In fact, Eric was well aware that he would need Mark more than ever now, due to the stress of the upcoming political campaign. Especially if he won and was granted access to real power. But he was scared that if Mark ever knew the full extent of his Mossad activities, Mark would leave him. Nevertheless, they all had a great dinner in a local restaurant that night with everyone getting pleasantly wasted on strong Israeli red wine. Jacob and Miriam also announced the date for their wedding that night at dinner. It was going to be a very big, grand wedding with lots of guests. This was not accidental. Both Jacob and

Miriam agreed that it would be positive political publicity for her son. A little high from the wine, Eric flippantly joked that it would be like the spectacles in the coliseum held for the masses by the caesars of ancient Rome. Nobody paid any attention to this remark.

Two days later, Mark and Eric arrived promptly for the 11 a.m. meeting. The campaign office was nothing fancy, located on the first floor of a somewhat dilapidated art deco building in a particularly shabby part of Tel Aviv.

Bo was waiting for them. He ushered them into the office and into a small conference room with a sturdy oval wooden table big enough to seat a dozen people. Mark could smell the dust in the room as he entered and sat. He assumed it hadn't been used in a while. Bo started by saying, "I think it's time I explain a little about the political campaign system here in Israel. You are going to have to make an important strategy decision very soon, whether you want to run as the head of your own new political party or the leader of an established one."

Eric, taking a minute to process this, replied, "I think joining an established party would increase my changes of a win."

Bo nodded in agreement saying, "Many existing parties would want a national hero like you in their ranks. Of course, we will have to see what is offered to you and if you agree with their existing platforms. I will contact them and say you are interested in possibly joining one."

Bo then took a breath and faced Eric, saying, "I believe I have your campaign slogan. And I hope you agree. It's something you said yourself when we met. The slogan should be, Israel First and Always!" The name hit Eric and Mark like a brick. They both agreed that it was the perfect slogan for a military hero's campaign. Eric loved the idea. Mark thought to himself, *The slogan worked in the US, so why not here? Maybe this guy knows what he is doing after all? Time will tell.*

Bo stood up to speak, saying, "The Maccabiah World Games start tomorrow, and I bought you both prime seats located in the middle of Teddy Stadium, in the first row of the ground floor next to the track. So everyone in the stadium will be able to see you from that location. I think it will be good exposure. I'm also a big supporter of the games. But I will not attend with you. My philosophy is to work in the background. Also, your four major opponents for the PM job will be there, including the current acting PM who wants to run for the office in his own right."

Bo was impressed with Eric's political savvy when Eric said, "Yes. I agree. Since the recent resignation of the Prime Minister and the upcoming elections, the more exposure I have, the better. And I guess there is no financial limitation on political publicity."

The Maccabiah Games are held every four years in Israel and are the equivalent of the Olympics for Jews around the world. They last about ten days and include dozens of Olympic style sporting events. Many non-Jews attend as well. It is considered the third largest sporting event in the world behind the Olympics and the FIFA World Cup. About 10,000 athletes attend. Some consider it a dry run to compete in the Olympics. Many sports events are held in Teddy Stadium located outside of Jerusalem, which can seat over 32,000 people. The rest are held throughout the country. The one major difference compared to the Olympics is its philosophy of kindness and gentleness. So, in addition to Olympic level competition, this translates to many events for young men and women, older people, and Paralympics for people with disabilities. Everyone can compete once they go through the registration process. In other words, the games are supposed to be fun for all—almost like a big Village Fair. The games have also become a prime recruiting ground for young athletes to immigrate to Israel. It is called making Aliyah or moving to Israel. This makes excellent sense, as the building blocks of any nation are healthy, athletic people.

Because Eric is already a national hero in Israel, when he entered Teddy Stadium to watch the Opening Ceremony and took his seat with Mark by his side, everyone turned to look and many clapped. It was not yet widely known that he had decided to enter the race for Prime Minister. Moreover, because of the central location of his seat at ground level, everyone in the stadium had no trouble seeing him. Bo had picked the seats himself to give Eric maximum exposure. As Eric entered the stadium, his Mossad training kicked in. Most people thought he was waving to them as he looked over the crowds and inhaled the thrill of his cheering fans. But really, he was visually checking the exits for possible escape routes in case of trouble and the number of Mossad agents embedded in the crowd. He counted eight agents but knew there must be more. He also noticed that there were exactly two dozen Shin Bet (Israeli Police) patrolling the periphery of the track area. Just beyond the brick and plaster stadium divider fence, the track area was further divided from the stands by two rows of somewhat flimsy metal fences—each about five feet (1.5m) long with a space between them. He did this visual review at every sporting event they attended. Moreover, Eric and Mark attended every game they could together, giving them exposure to the nation as a gay couple.

Towards the middle of the Maccabiah Games, on day five, the wheelchair race was held for two dozen wheelchair bound athletes. It was one lap around the sizable stadium track. It was a beautiful but hot day and the stadium was full to capacity.

Eric and Mark had taken their seats to watch the event. By now, the press was constantly following Eric everywhere. This was not an accident, but arranged by his campaign manager, Bo, who was watching the games on TV.

As the wheelchair race started, Eric stood and leaned his elbows on top of the brick and plaster fence dividing the stands from the stadium floor to get a better view. The press was in the press box with a few photographers and mobile camera men on the roof of a van following the race up close. But most press were not paying too much attention to events. Mark was seated next to Eric, staring off at the beautiful sky and not particularly following the race either. While standing, Eric's eagle eye noticed that one of the race participants was falling further and further behind the others at the track's farthest point. He realized the contestant was in trouble. Spontaneously, he easily grasped the top of the stadium fence with both hands and hurled his feet and body over it like a gymnast, landing with both feet on the floor of the stadium. He quickly jogged between the spaces in the metal fences to the straggler who had by then completely stopped to catch his breath. As Eric approached him, he saw someone who looked like a teenager in a wheelchair looking really winded and sweating. So, he just casually said, "My name is Eric. I see you're getting tired. Mind if I push you so we can finish the race together?"

To which the teenage racer responded, "Yes, please. Thanks for the help. I was getting a little winded. The course is longer than I thought. And this hot weather doesn't help. My name is Ofer. Nice to meet you."

With that, Eric got behind Ofer's wheelchair, grasped the handles and pushed with all his strength—to get up to running speed. The stadium announcer recognized Eric and announced the unexpected helper's name as retired Colonel Eric Jansen from the Israeli Special Forces. They finished last but they finished. And that's what mattered. When they crossed the finish line, the stadium exploded in applause—yelling Eric's name. Eric and Ofer said goodbye to one another as Eric turned to walk back to his seat. However, the press corp went crazy trying to get a statement from Eric, who by this time was stopped cold on the field halfway back to his seat surrounded by press and fans leaving the bleachers trying to congratulate him or touch him. The Shin Bet police were barely able to control the crowd of fans. Finally, someone in the press corp handed him a microphone so Eric could make a statement. All he said was, "Israel leaves no one behind! And I have decided to run for Prime Minister to make sure of it! Israel First and Always!" That was it. More of his fans flooded onto the field, overturning the meager metal barricades separating the sporting tracks from the stands to try to congratulate him, touch him or get close to him.

Mark was stunned when he saw this happening. But Mark also realized the danger to his partner with so many thousands of people rushing towards him on the stadium field—albeit well intentioned. He thought Eric and others in the crowd could be trampled to death. So he quickly called Bo on speed dial. Bo picked up instantly saying he was watching on TV what was happening. They both agreed Eric was in danger. Mark, thinking quickly, told Bo to call the stadium announcer and tell him to start playing Hava Nagila—the Israeli national folk dance song—also called a hora. Bo hesitated, but Mark now told him in a tone Staff Sergeants use when ordering their new recruits. "Just do it!" Bo ended the call and immediately called his contact in the announcer's box with the odd request. About a minute later, the hora music started playing over the stadium loudspeakers. And what do Israeli's do when they hear that song? They start to dance! This folk dance requires men and or women to form a circle with intertwining arms. It is very similar to the Greek and Turkish folk dances. Within minutes the whole stadium was dancing the hora—including Eric. Several circles almost immediately formed. The largest circle had Eric and Mark—who had run on to the field to help his partner if needed—dancing around the wheelchair race participants in the circle's center who were clapping their raised hands to the music. Thus, the dangerous crowd stampede ended just as quickly as it began. The stadium had turned into one big dance festival!

And not a minute too soon. As it happened, one of the first fans who broke through the Shin Bet police line protecting Eric was a young woman who grabbed Eric's shirt, tearing it open. But upon hearing the dance music he intertwined his arm with hers and said to her, "Let's dance." Surprised, but instantly agreeing, she intertwined her arm with the person behind her and so on and so on. After about twenty minutes of dancing, singing, and laughing, Mark asked Eric, "You ok? I think it's time to leave." Eric happily nodded in agreement and they both slipped out of the celebrating stadium to their car. After Eric departed, the crowd slowly dispersed back to the stands with a possible crisis averted—no casualties!

In the car driving home, Eric turned to Mark, saying, "I don't have to ask. The music was your out of the box idea. It probably saved my life and the lives of others. Thank you." Mark said nothing. He just looked straight ahead, feeling a bit lightheaded about what just happened. What could he say. He was realizing that politics could be very dangerous. He asked himself, *What did they get themselves into?* Nevertheless, years later, many people still said that was the day Eric Jansen won the race for prime minister.

After watching everything on national TV, Bo knew they were all safe. He didn't call Eric or Mark that night, but waited until the next morning. He also waited to collect his thoughts since he was furious that Eric pulled a stunt like that— almost killing himself and others in the process. He called Eric the next morning, trying to control the irritation in his voice, to calmly but firmly ask Eric if both he and Mark could please attend a meeting in the campaign office ASAP. They of course agreed. When Bo hung up, Mark turned to Eric and said, "I think we're going to get a spanking?" Eric just chuckled a little at Mark's remark but said nothing.

At the meeting later, Bo didn't want any small talk before they all sat around the old conference table. He calmly started the meeting by looking directly at Eric with his steely blue eyes saying, "Welcome. I just want to know what part of my instructions not to talk to the press or do anything publicly without my approval first, didn't you understand?"

Before Eric could respond, Jacob walked—actually more like burst—into the meeting and sat down. He had a big grin on his face, saying, "I want to compliment everyone. Yesterday was the best political publicity stunt I have ever seen! The whole country saw it and I will make sure through my TV station and streaming channels it will be seen again and again. It's even been picked up by the international press. Eric, you played it flawlessly. And Mark, Bo told me it was your idea to play the dance music. I want to compliment you both for brilliantly working together by instructing the stadium announcer to play the hora dance music to stop the crowd stampede towards Eric. What a beautiful team we are becoming!"

With that said, the tense mood of the meeting changed to one of positive energy and a can-do spirit, all wanting to figure out the next steps for the campaign. Mark was quietly impressed with Jacob's leadership skills while Eric put on his Mossad inscrutable spy-face so no one could tell what he was thinking. Bo, smiling from Jacob's compliment, said, "Well, I think the next step is to get a security detail for Eric and Mark."

Jacob immediately agreed saying, "I have two people for it. But Mark, at this point you will have to self-fund it." After what happened yesterday, Mark just nodded in agreement. Jacob further said, "But listen, I believe I have a big backer for your campaign. He saw what happened in the stadium and wants to meet you both. But he wants to remain anonymous. I set up a meeting at my Jerusalem house two days from now at 10 a.m. But please be there 30 minutes early so I can brief you. I need to go. I just stopped in to congratulate you all. I think the campaign is off to a strong start. Regardless of what happens at this upcoming meeting, it will be much easier to get campaign donors to fund it now."

Before anyone could say anything else, Eric spoke, saying, "I just want to make one thing perfectly clear. I did not help this guy initially as a publicity stunt. I saw him in trouble and before I knew it, I was over the fence helping him. I would have done it for anyone. It was dumb luck that it turned into something positive for my campaign. But yes, I did take the opportunity to announce my candidacy once I saw where it was going. And yes, I am very glad no one got hurt. Also I want to make sure, Bo, that you are aware that I want to run my campaign by the book. The way I plan to govern if I win. No illegal contributions or side deals."

Bo immediately responded, "And that is why you pay me. So there are no accidents. And events are thoroughly planned as much as possible ahead of time." Mark was glad to hear this clearcut statement by Eric, but sensed that Jacob didn't take Eric's statement seriously. It was almost as if he knew something that Mark didn't. Bo continued, "Therefore, in my opinion your announcement yesterday of your candidacy for PM in the stadium was a strong first step but not enough to clinch it. So let's get to work." At this point Jacob got up with a slight nod to everyone and left the meeting.

After Jacob departed, Bo said, "Mark and Eric, I want you both to be present as much as possible at all the LBGTQ events and organization meetings in Israel including marching in the June Pride Parade. I have prepared a list of upcoming events for you to attend. The LBGTQ market represents about 7% of the voting public and we will need every vote. Eric, because of your military background, I want you also to focus on veterans organizations and-"

Eric interrupted Bo by saying, "I also want to focus on the Israeli settlers in Judea and Samaria. There are about 600,000 of them."

Bo responded, "Yes, I agree, and they have a very high voter turnout."

CHAPTER THREE

PRAYER SHAWLS AND YARMULKES

Before another word was said, there was knock at the door. Bo yelled, "Come in. It's open." To everyone's surprise, there stood Saul Jacoby, the leader of the largest political party in Israel.

He quietly said, "May I have a seat? I have a proposal for Eric."

After taking a seat at the table, he continued, "I saw what happened in the stadium along with most of my party members and we were impressed. You have the leadership, communication skills, military background and good looks to lead our party and be the next Prime Minister. In other words, you're a hero and the country needs a hero. However, what you don't have is enough time to build your own political party before the next election, let alone govern if you win. I did a survey of our party members before I came here, and they all agreed you would be perfect to lead our party. According to that poll I am sure you will win our party primary. So I would like to offer you the leadership of our party and thus the PM job when you help us get majority control of the Knesset. I don't believe you can do it without us. Especially since you are a gay married couple. The ultra-Orthodox Haredi Jews will never vote for you."

Everyone at the table was stunned. Bo spoke first, when he said, "Don't you mean you can't get majority control of the Knesset without Eric?"

Saul replied, "Let's not quibble. We both need each other, that's why I'm here. We will leave the present coalition, forcing an election by law in 45 days, and together we will not need a coalition of parties to govern. As you know, all we need is 61 seats out of 120. But we prefer to get much more if we can."

Eric replied, "What about the present acting PM? Isn't he the leader of your party now and wants to run for PM?"

To this, Saul quietly said while looking firmly into Eric's eyes, "Our acting PM is a strong number two but the consensus within the party is that he doesn't have what it takes to be a number one. I will ease him out if you accept."

Bo, now, interjected, "Is there anything else you want as part of this deal? Let's hear it now."

Saul paused for a moment before he said, "Yes, there is quid pro quo. I want you to support me as the next President of the Knesset to help you govern. As you know the President of the Knesset's role in Israel is similar to the Speaker of the House in the United States, and you will need me in that role." Now, they all turned to Eric to hear from him.

Eric thought to himself while listening to Saul, *This guy is going to double cross a longtime associate in his party for the sake of his own political advancement. He will do it to me someday too. I should throw him out right now. But he could be right. I may need him and his party to get elected.* So, Eric responded with his most non-committal stare while keeping his real feelings under control, "This is a most gracious and exciting offer. I need a day to decide. I will give you my answer in 24 hours. However, before we finalize anything we need to sit down together to make sure we are on the same page regarding some political items on your party's platform."

With that, Saul gave a small nod to everyone and stood to leave, saying, "Agreed. We'll speak soon. Bo has my number. Have a good day."

There was dead silence for a minute after he left the room. Then they all started to talk at once. Finally, Bo silenced Mark and Eric saying, "That was too easy. Although he is correct. It will be easier to join an established political party, especially the single largest one. It's a center right party. I don't think you and he will have any issues that can't be worked through."

Eric replied, "I know the party. There are just one or two

things I might want to change on their platform. You're right it would be a good fit. I think."

Bo added, "Whatever you decide, I will make it work for you. He was right about one thing. The Haredi Jews will never vote for a homosexual—committed to each other in marriage or not. It is your political weakness. So in order to soften their objection and anybody else's, I need you to make a concerted approach to the religious orthodox community in the country, regardless of what you decide about your political party affiliation. You can start with a visit to the Western Wall tomorrow. Let's set up a photo shoot of you both praying there."

In response to what just happened, while staring into the middle of the empty table, Eric said loudly, "Wow, I have a lot to think about." Mark, however, could tell Eric said it more to himself than to anyone else in the room.

Bo sensing that indeed, Eric was correct, said, "Let's break the meeting for today. I have a lot to follow up and Eric needs some time to think." As they all left for the day, Eric thought to himself, *I need to discuss all this with Jacob.*

On the way home Eric was very quiet, thinking about his decisions and not speaking a word to Mark. Arriving home, they found two security guards waiting for them outside. Jacob had meant what he said. The two men were professional bodyguards. As Eric and Mark got out of their car in front of their home, the security guards introduced themselves as Ariel and Kfir. Eric was polite but occupied with his own thoughts, so after the brief introduction Eric and Mark quickly entered their home. Eric, now, did something which Mark hadn't seen Eric do in years, and then only to destress. As soon as the front door closed behind them, Eric started to disrobe, leaving a trail of clothes while walking through the house to their very private pool in their backyard, hidden from all viewers by high walls covered in flowering vines. He dove in naked and started doing laps while deep in thought without saying a word to Mark. There was a time when Mark would have slipped into the pool after him to make love. But not that day. Mark knew that Eric was under pressure to make the right political decisions and needed some time alone to think.

Unbeknownst to Mark, while in the pool Eric had a PTSD (Post Traumatic Stress Disorder) relapse. Eric thought he was again in the Egyptian Nile River swimming, holding his Israeli Special Force buddy to keep his head above water with one arm while climbing to safety on the riverbank—only to discover when he turned around that almost half of his buddy's body had been severed and eaten by a Nile crocodile. The bite had been so fierce and quick and the gunfire around them so intensely loud that Eric had not been aware it when it happened. The massive amount of his buddy's blood alerted even more of these Nile monster crocs who were hurriedly closing in on his location. In the pool, Eric thought that he was once again carrying what was left of his friend to the helicopter pick up point. Eric luckily grabbed the edge of the gutter surrounding the pool to steady himself. He stood there motionless, feeling frozen in the hot sun and looking at the side of the pool but not seeing it for about five minutes. Like the day in the Nile, he was feeling surprised, terrified, shameful and guilty for letting this happen to a colleague and friend. What allowed him to get control of himself was also the memory of his orders to the gunners as he climbed into the helicopter to shoot to kill every crocodile in the river, knowing full well that only one killed his friend while the others were collateral damage. The image of dozens of crocodiles being torn apart by machine gun fire in revenge somehow calmed him, letting him get control of himself again and allowing his episode to pass. Eric knew he couldn't tell anyone what just occurred for fear of having to step aside from the election. Mark was busy inside the house and totally unaware of this incident. This recollection was one of many close calls Eric had endured during his military career. But, after mandatory counseling, he had been cleared by a military psychologist and both he and Mark felt that he had been cured of any PTSD. Thus, Jacob Kurtz and his friend, Sam Reichman, now Director of the Mossad, had his medical records sealed. So, after this disturbing episode, he finished swimming his laps, feeling politically safe that his PTSD medical history would never be revealed.

About an hour later, Eric emerged from their pool nude and dripping wet with droplets of water slowly trickling down his hard muscled frame. He walked into the house with only a towel around his waist, saying to Mark, "I have made my decision of what to do. I don't need Jacob's advice." He paused, then adding that he was starving. Mark had anticipated this and had prepared tuna fish sandwiches for a late lunch. Mark could tell that his partner, still one of the most handsome men in Israel, seemed at peace. As a Mossad operative, Eric had long been trained to hide his true emotions. The only difference in Eric's appearance since they first met was that he had changed his hair style, cutting his long blond hair that he had worn pulled tight with a rubber band behind his head to the current shorter version of his hair, just touching the tops of his ears. Therefore, Mark was oblivious to the emotional instability of his beloved partner or how the stress of the Prime Minister's position would affect Eric. Moreover, sitting on a kitchen stool at the kitchen table, all Eric's appetites returned with gusto. So, when they finished eating, Mark knew immediately what came next by the way Eric looked at him. They both felt the heat rising between them.

Since Mark was the much older partner, he made it a point to almost never be the first to instigate love making. It was his personal rule. But for now, they could not restrain themselves from making love and stayed in bed together for the rest of the afternoon. Approaching evening, Eric turned to Mark and said, "I'm hungry again. Let's go to that little fish restaurant overlooking the ocean in Haifa that we both love so much. We can sit outside and look at the sea. I'll let everyone know my political decision when I am good and ready. No more talk of politics tonight." When they left for the restaurant, the two security guards who had been outside their house followed in a separate car at a discreet distance.

Indeed, at dinner with the security guards almost out of sight, the conversation was mostly about archeology and their previous earth-shaking discoveries, such as the royal jewels of King Herod in a park outside of Jerusalem; the lost plunder of Egypt taken by Moses which they found in the Negev; and the lost Temple treasure found by the correct deciphering of the famous Copper Scroll. It was fun for both of them to walk down memory lane. But before the dinner was over, Eric was also curious about Mark's strong metaphysical skills, or what Mark called his hunches, that led them to their archeological successes. So he asked Mark, "Have you had any recent metaphysical episodes?"

To which Mark answered, "No, not really. I think my sensitivity to metaphysical things is triggered by my surroundings. For instance in King Tut's tomb in Egypt or in the ancient valley in front of the burning bush phenomena on Mount Karkom in the Negev. I have not had any metaphysical episodes since then nor do I want anymore. In fact, the only treasure I have found recently is sitting in front of me—you." Mark always knew what to say to Eric. He could tell that Eric seemed to emotionally melt in front of him. They both were still deeply in love after all these years, and that night easily fell asleep together in each other's arms. However, there was something that Mark noticed about his partner at dinner. Eric's eating habits had changed from eating only fish or chicken to almost exclusively eating meat—and he preferred it cooked rare. Luckily, their favorite fish restaurant also had a meat section on the menu.

The next day they awoke so early after a good night's sleep that they decided to leave for their scheduled photoshoot praying at the Western Wall in Jerusalem earlier than planned while the security guards followed at a discreet distance. They arrived early enough to take a stroll around the city beforehand. They entered through the Jaffa Gate and took their time sauntering through the narrow city streets to the Western Wall on the other side of the city. Unfortunately, all the shops were closed at that hour. So they had to content themselves with looking into the shop windows. The streets were almost empty as the sun began to rise.

That's when they heard a call for help in Hebrew and what sounded like men fighting around the corner. As Mark and Eric ran to see if they could help, they saw three Arab teenagers attacking an old Jewish man who was on the floor being kicked and punched. He was still bravely holding onto his wallet with one hand and his prayer shawl in the other, preventing both from being stolen or damaged. He had a long grayish-white beard, was dressed in black and wore a black yarmulka (Jewish skull cap) on his head. Eric yelled in perfect Arabic at the youths to stop and get the hell away. Instead of fleeing, all three turned to face him and pulled out knives. That was definitely the wrong decision on their part. Instantly, Eric jumped in the middle of the group in fighting mode, disarming all of them in minutes. Then, unusual for him, he unclenched his fists and slapped one of the would be muggers so hard across the face that the teenager almost fell to his knees. That startled them all enough to flee. They were gone in seconds, leaving their knives on the ground. While this was happening, Mark was helping the old man to his feet and asking in Hebrew if he was okay. The security guards arrived seconds later with guns drawn.

Mark and Eric could see that old man was still shaken, but said he was fine as Mark helped him to his feet. The teenagers hadn't had time to do him any real damage. He introduced himself as Rabbi Itzhak Sofer and thanked them both for rescuing him from being mugged. Eric and Mark also introduced themselves. Rabbi Sofer observed that Eric had not really used his full strength in the fight. Eric just turned to him and laughingly said, "I didn't want to kill anybody so early in the morning, especially since we are on our way to pray to God at the Western Wall."

Rabbi Sofer thought for a second to process what he had just heard, questioning whether it had been said in jest or deadly truth. Then, ignoring Eric's last remark, he said, "I am also on my way there for early morning prayers."

Mark interjected, "So let's walk together. We can be your protection."

The Rabbi replied, "Excellent idea. I usually walk with a group of my friends, but today I came alone." Regaining his balance further, and with a twinkle in his eye, he added, "By the way, after what I just saw regarding those security guards of yours with their guns still drawn. Are you sure they are protecting you? Or are you protecting them?" With that remark they all started to laugh, including the guards who had overheard it.

It only took them another five minutes to arrive at the open air prayer plaza in front of the Western Wall, a remnant of the outer wall of the Jewish Holy Temple compound. As they walked, Rabbi Sofer asked why they were praying there today. Eric responded truthfully, "I am running for prime minister and my campaign manager thought it would be a good idea to be photographed praying at the Wall like so many other politicians. Especially since Mark and I are gay and married."

This answer did not offend Rabbi Sofer in the least. He was used to dealing with Jewish secularists as well as the strictly orthodox. So he simply asked, "Do you both believe in God?"

To which both Eric and Mark replied together in unison, "Yes."

The Rabbi then continued, "I can see that you are good men, and a strong friendship between men, even gay friends, is perfectly acceptable in the eyes of God."

Both Mark and Eric really didn't comprehend what the Rabbi had just told them. But he had shrewdly given them a political workaround to approach orthodox Jews in the country for their votes. Or, in other words, in the view of the orthodox Jews, a non-ordained gay marriage without sex is just two male friends living together as roommates. This breaks no religious prohibitions.

When they arrived at the prayer area in front of the Western Wall, Rabbi Sofer looked at his new friends and said, "Here, take these." He then pulled two black yarmulkes from his pocket and gave them to his new friends, saying, "You can't pray without them. It's my present to you both." He then turned and walked towards the other orthodox Jews praying. One strange thing that caught Mark's eye about their new friend was that as Rabbi Sofer walked into the crowd of orthodox Jews, they all nodded their heads in respect as he passed.

The photo session showing Eric and Mark wearing their yarmulkes while standing and praying at the Western Wall went off without a hitch. The press loved it, garnering much publicity for Eric's race to become prime minister. Eric had prayed there many times before as a member of the Israel's armed forces, so he knew the etiquette required. He softly uttered the traditional prayers in Hebrew with his head bent and one hand touching the Western Wall. Following tradition, before he started praying he stuffed a little handwritten prayer to God into a crack in the Western Wall. Free note paper, pencils and a table on which to write were available as they entered the plaza.

However, it was Mark's first time praying at the Western Wall. He had passed it several times while visiting Jerusalem but never stopped to pray. It is hard to miss since it is still part of the surrounding outside wall of the Temple Mount and is

62 feet (19m) tall and 1600 feet (488m) long. He basically followed Eric's lead, including touching the Wall with one hand while bowing his head and praying. As he approached the sacred Western Wall and stood at its base to pray, he also was enveloped with the spiritual power of the place. Many people have said they felt the same sensation standing before it. However, when he laid his hand upon the ancient, cold, stone surface, duplicating Eric's movements as his guide, he could have sworn he heard the sound of a trumpet or horn. It sounded so beautiful and forceful that he backed away from the Wall, removing his hand from touching the Wall and looked over his shoulder to see if anyone was blowing a trumpet. All he saw was Eric praying next to him and the press corp busy snapping photos and recording videos of them. Moreover, he realized that as soon as he removed his hand the Wall, the sound of the trumpet stopped. He thought he would try touching the Wall again to see if he had been hallucinating. Sure enough, when he touched the wall, he heard the trumpet again. But this time, listening more closely, he could swear the sound was coming from underneath the stone floor of the prayer plaza. Getting control of his thoughts, he asked himself, *What's underneath here?* Though he appeared to be deep in prayer, keeping his head bowed, he was focused solely on the sound of the trumpet. He felt the strong curiosity of an archeologist

wanting to get to the bottom of this phenomenon. But Mark knew they were in the throes of a tough political campaign and he shouldn't do anything to impede the campaign or take the spotlight off his partner. He decided not to tell Eric about this experience and play it very cool.

Afterwards, they both walked slowly back through the now awakened and lively streets of Jerusalem. They decided to spend the rest of the day relaxing in the city. Mark, curious to hear an archeologist's point of view, asked Eric what was underneath the stone floor of the prayer plaza. Eric casually replied, "Lots of tunnels. The part of the Western Wall that we have just touched and seen extends approximately 62 feet (19m) above the modern prayer plaza in front of the Wall. However, the total height of the wall was originally much higher since we know from written records that the Romans knocked over at least another 10 to 15 feet (4.6m) of it. Much of that top layer of stones can be seen in the tunnels below the modern street level, lying on the original street pavers. So the total height of the outside wall of the Temple Mount was about 105 feet (32m) before its destruction in Roman times. This leaves a gap of about 40 feet (12m) below the modern day floor to the ancient street level. Perhaps you should take a trip to visit the newly excavated tunnels underneath the prayer plaza one day."

Mark answered, "Perhaps I will." What Mark didn't say was that it was now his priority to visit them. He had developed a hunch that something important was in those tunnels and he wanted to discover it. This was his first hunch in years. But he didn't want to mention anything to Eric due to their focus on his political campaign. He tried hard to convince himself that everything else could wait until Eric was elected.

The City of Jerusalem is an archeologist's paradise with so many different layers of civilization built atop one another. Since Eric was a certified archeologist specializing in Biblical history, he was able to explain to Mark exactly what they were seeing. Mark loved to listen to him. As they walked, Mark commented on how clean the city was kept and how the Israelis had cleverly repaired and fitted all the different styles into something cohesive and beautiful. Eric replied, "Did you know that just before the city's destruction in 70 CE, it was the cleanest and thereby the healthiest city in the ancient world for its time because of its extensive underground water and sewage system?"

Mark replied that he had read something about that, but he then changed the subject, saying to Eric, "You know, if being Prime Minister doesn't work out, then you could be a professor of archeology at some university."

Eric replied with a smile, "You mean like Indiana Jones?"

Mark instantly and forcefully retorted, "No, not all. No more dangerous missions! Period!" Eric, taken aback at Mark's strong tone, just nodded in agreement but didn't verbally agree.

To change the subject again, while standing in a somewhat less busy corner of Jerusalem's vibrant street scene, Eric said, "I think it's time for me to call Jacob and tell him my decision. You should listen to this." He called Jacob on his cellphone, connecting to him seconds later, saying with no introduction, "I think you already know that Saul Jacoby visited our campaign headquarters just after you left. You probably advised him to make the offer. So, I want to tell you my decision. I think Saul Jacoby was correct. Due to the short time frame before the next election, instead of establishing my own political party, I would welcome the opportunity to become the leader of Israel's largest party and their nominee for Prime Minister."

Jacob, not surprised by this decision said, "Excellent. I expected you to say that. Now call Bo to make it official so that he can contact Saul and formulate your election strategy." Pausing for a moment to think, Jacob then added, "Based on your decision, I want you to meet one more person that can help your campaign. I will set up a meeting for tomorrow in my house in Jerusalem at 10 a.m. with this other person. Please bring Mark." With that, Jacob abruptly ended the call as his style. Eric immediately called Bo to tell him the news. When

Jacob Kurtz ended his call with Eric, he thought to himself how politically insightful, even shrewd, Eric had become. Or had Eric always been like that and he hadn't noticed? The first thing Bo told Eric to do when he heard of Eric's decision was to join the party online as a member. Eric joined that night so that in the future he could be put on the party's list of candidates for the Knesset in the upcoming election.

CHAPTER FOUR

NEW ALLIANCES

The next morning, Jacob's surprise political backer for Eric's campaign arrived on schedule earlier than Eric and Mark. Their meeting place was Jacob's second home in Israel—a sleek, ultra modern house in the new part of Jerusalem covered with white limestone that glistened in the sunlight—a very appropriate home for a man whose wealth totaled almost a billion dollars. This location and earlier timing of their meeting gave Jacob and his guest, Alexander ben Halevi, the ability to discuss things in private. Alexander was the head of the ben Halevi family clan. He was almost 70 years old with a full head of slightly graying hair and a clean shaven face. He wore custom made black trousers, an open collar white shirt and a pair of suede loafers. While he gave off a very relaxed image, he was masking a mind like a steel trap. He now lived in Israel since his family's business headquarters located in Bagdad for centuries was forcibly closed under Saddam Hussain's regime. Even Jacob was impressed with

Alexander's family wealth. Jacob's research revealed that the ben Halevi clan had been rich for centuries. For example, he discovered that during the Crusades the ben Halevi clan was the primary seller of alcohol to the Muslims as well as provider of banking services to the Christians—both respectively forbidden by their willing customer's religions—making them a fortune. He also found that their trading prowess was legendary, going back even further than the crusades. The only reason Jacob was able to learn these small bits and pieces of their history was from information supplied by the Israeli Intelligence services which he oversaw.

And now the head of this hugely wealthy, powerful and prominent clan was sitting across from him having coffee and a biscuit for breakfast. Alexander spoke first, "I want to thank you for inviting me to breakfast so we can discuss our interest in Eric Jansen's campaign for Prime Minister. My wife and I saw him in Teddy Stadium during the Maccabiah Games the other day and were very impressed with his communication and leadership skills. And the more research we did on him, the more impressed we became. No question about it. He is a national hero." Jacob tightly smiled in response, nodding his acknowledgment to this opening comment. Alexander continued, "I am aware of Israel's extremely strict political campaign funding laws. However, I am here to possibly fund

Eric Jansen's campaign to the extent legally possible. But also, I would like to offer our help with anything else that he may need during the campaign and while in office. But first I need to know if he can be controlled. The reason I ask this is that we have discovered something in the Negev desert which will take years to develop, cost billions and is very likely to have environmental development problems."

Jacob was stunned. He thought he knew everything that was happening of importance in the country. He replied, "First, yes, we can control Eric. If it is for the betterment and strengthening of Israel, I am sure he would be for it. But secondly, I have not heard of this project, and I thought I knew about everything important happening in Israel."

Alexander answered, "I am glad you feel so strongly about Mr. Jansen. Yes, this project will strengthen the economy of Israel. And I am not surprised you know nothing about it because we worked directly with the former prime minister who was sworn to secrecy. We now wish to work with the next PM."

Alexander took a short silent mental break, collecting himself, then continued, "There is one more reason I am sitting here. I have four sons. The three older ones work for me and are doing very well in our operations. But my youngest son only cares about archeology and music. He lives and breathes both. Since he heard about me possibly funding Mr. Jansen's campaign, he has been begging me to introduce him to Eric Jansen and his partner, Mark Cohn. We love him dearly, but his mother and I are afraid he will not amount to anything. Truthfully, he can be so headstrong sometimes." Jacob looked perplexed at this last statement. So Alexander continued, "I know it is unusual to ask this now. Let's wait until Eric Jansen and Mark Cohn arrive and I will explain it all further. I also asked my son to meet us here too. I thought he and Mark Cohn could talk privately while we discuss things with Mr. Jansen." Jacob, of course, agreed. But he liked being in control and he was getting nervous that this was no longer the case.

Five minutes later the doorbell rang. It was Alexander's twenty year old son. Again, Jacob pressed his wireless automatic release button to open his front door. After everyone introduced themselves, Alexander asked Jacob if his son could wait in the room next door until they finished with their meeting. Jacob readily agreed. Alexander then told his son he would send Mark Cohn in to meet him as soon as he arrived. Not three minutes later, both Eric and Mark walked through the automatically opened front door and into Jacob's library with their curiosity aroused to meet this mystery campaign backer. Immediately, Alexander stood to greet them while Jacob made the introductions. They all agreed to use informal first names.

The first thing Jacob said was that Alexander's son was an amateur archeologist waiting in the next room, anxious to meet both of them but especially Mark. He asked Mark if he wouldn't mind going into the next room to talk with Alexander's son about archeology while they spoke politics here. Mark said, "No problem. I would enjoy speaking with him." He then promptly left the room, thinking to himself, *Good, I don't have to sit through a boring political meeting.*

Sitting down, Alexander explained in detail why he wanted to fund Eric's campaign. "I will fund the whole thing up to what's legally permissible, but I need someone as prime minister who will support my Negev project. I will tell you now that there won't be any more camel races there."

Eric blinked, saying, "I guess you researched me."

To which Alexander replied, "Yes, I do my homework. But let me continue. Until now, geologists thought that what we call the Ramon Crater in the middle of the Negev was actually a gash in the earth's crust made by looser soil underneath giving way and thus cracking the harder limestone surface, creating something that looks like a meteor crater to the general public. But to the trained geologists eye it looks more like the Grand Canyon in the US. However, due to our recent geological explorations using the state of the art equipment that can detect much deeper and more accurate geological anomalies than ever before, we were able to detect and verify commercial quantities of copper and gold with the strong possibilities of future commercial rare earth discoveries as well. The concentration and proximity of these minerals to each other tell us that there was indeed a meteor impact about three million years ago. Previous geologists missed this using less advanced exploratory equipment. Or in other words, we found the mother lode! And here is something that will interest you, Eric, with your archeology background. The ancient copper deposits mined by King Solomon and the ancient Egyptians at the southern tip of the Negev were actually created when the meteor hit, hurtling these much smaller copper deposits through the earth away from impact."

Both Eric and Jacob sat silently trying to process what they were hearing. Alexander, however, kept on talking, "But here is why I need your commitment to this project as PM. The cost to bring this mine to fruition will be about 5 billion dollars or about 18 billion shekels. I will fund half of it myself and have already arranged a consortium of backers for the other half. I also will have controlling interest in the project. It will take three to five years to open and make this mine profitable. This time frame will be closer to three years if I have a PM who supports it. I need someone to ease the license permitting process, as well as to deal with the Israeli

Land Authority and various ministries. And let us not forget that the mine is in the middle of the Judean Desert Nature Preserve which means the Environmental Protection Ministry will fight it tooth and nail. We need a Prime Minister who will cut through all that and make it happen. The good news is that it will enormously strengthen the Israeli economy with thousands of permanent high paying jobs and make the country a world player in the global commodity market. Also we would like a twenty year tax break once the mine starts to produce. Thus, the government becomes our partner."

Eric was no fool. He knew exactly what Alexander was asking. He thought to himself, *He wants to pollute the land, take all the profits and then walk away without any penalties or clean up.*

So Eric waited a couple of minutes, making the two other gentleman in the meeting somewhat anxious before thoughtfully responding, "I will support you under the following conditions. First, you must go through the normal governmental transparent bidding process for a project this size. I, of course will make sure that you get the winning bid. Second, in the final analysis, the Israeli government owns 40% of the mine and receives 40% of all profits. The profits will be audited monthly by a government appointed auditor. Third, I believe mining projects need a great deal of water in production. Any water pipes run into the Mediterranean or Gulf of Eilat or Dead Sea must be government inspected, government approved and environmentally safe. Fourth, any clean up of environmental damage must be borne by the mine or if the mine closes, then by the mine owners. Fifth, a governing Mine Council will be established to manage the mine. The government must have a third of the seats on it. The actual number of seats can be determined later. Six, at this point I cannot guarantee the length of any tax reduction or any tax abatement at all. If you agree to all my points then I will fight with all my political strength as PM to get this project done on the terms agreed upon."

In response, Alexander just sat there studying Eric's face and looking into his eyes. Alexander felt he recognized the eyes of a cold blooded killer staring back at him. Only then did he feel really assured that Eric would make a formidable Prime Minister for the State of Israel against its insanely murderous neighbors. Eric intentionally thought this was the time to show Alexander exactly who he was. So, he had allowed Alexander to see his black side—but just for a moment.

After a long five minutes, with the tension in the room palpable, Alexander, anticipating this negotiation, simply said without blinking or showing any feeling, "I can do 35%, not 40% across the board for the government share. All else I agree to. I strongly believe our new mining techniques will keep costs down and environmental damage to a minimum."

Breaking the tension, all three men stood to shake hands in a close circle. All smiling, looking at one another. Repeating the word, "Agreed." However, to the outside casual observer their smiles would have seemed more like snarls. Alexander added, "Of course, you now have our complete financial backing as well as anything else you may need to win and stay in office."

Jacob then interjected, "No need to tell Bo or anyone else about this agreement." All three verbally answered, "Yes. Also agreed." Jacob added, "I am getting married soon and would like to invite you and your wife to the wedding."

Alexander surprised both men when he replied, "Yes. We would be happy to attend. And mazel tov to you both, since I know it's Eric's mother that you are marrying. Remember, I told you I do my homework." On this note, Alexander decided to say goodbye to his son next door and leave.

.ܓܨܠܨܩ.

OLD SOULS

Earlier, Mark had left the meeting to enter the room next door. As he opened the door, he saw a young man about twenty years old sitting on a sofa who immediately stood to greet him. Mark's first impression of the young man was that he seemed to be a bit short but well muscled and clean shaven with penetrating dark brown eyes and dark brown hair. The young man spoke first saying, "You must be Mark Cohn. I recognize you from the photographs on your books and press appearances. My name is Aaron ben Halevi and I have been looking forward to meeting you. But please call me Ari—everyone does."

Mark responded, "Yes, good to meet you too." As they shook hands Mark experienced—like a jolt—a surprisingly strong metaphysical episode. It was his first episode in a long time. The room suddenly vanished and changed in front of his eyes to a vision of swirling black smoke with an acidic smell that burnt his nostrils. He felt the intense heat of searing fire and heard the terrorized screams of dying men, women and children. Then appearing to him through the smoke was the Holy Temple itself on the Temple Mount, still in all its glory but in flames. He also noticed a man dressed in the royal blue robes with its edges fringed in tiny gold bells. The man was standing with his back to Mark, staring up at the burning Temple. The man quickly turned and looked over his soldier straight at Mark, clearly showing his face. It felt to Mark like this vision took forever, but as Ari released Mark's handshake after just a couple of moments, the vision instantly vanished too. Recovering from this without missing a beat except for an inhaled half breath, Mark simply said, "You must be an old soul. I have never in my life met someone with as much hypersensitivity to metaphysics as myself." Mark secretly fought back an urge to bow and kiss the young man's hand because the face he saw in his vision was the older bearded version of the Ari's face. Mark instinctively knew this was the way to greet the High Priest of the Holy Temple.

However, it was as if Ari sensed what Mark had just seen when Ari simply replied, "Yes. I see an old soul in you too."

Both men, regardless of the difference in age and backgrounds, knew they were instant friends—on the same wavelength as if they were greeting an old friend they hadn't seen in a long while. Ari stood smiling warmly, looking at Mark. They both decided to sit and talk, feeling a sense of meeting again but for the first time—if that was possible. During this conversation Mark also sensed a great deal of insecurity in his new acquaintance, which Ari hid very well to most people. After a while Ari said to Mark, "Archeologist be damned. You are the most famous treasure hunter in the country, if not the world."

This flattered Mark deeply, but he tried to minimize it by replying, "Thank you, but I have discovered there are a lot of laws regulating that sort of thing. I almost went to jail more than once." They both half smiled at this. Young Ari felt that he already knew by the feigned, bashful tone of his friend Mark's reply how to handle him! Mark was also very impressed to learn that as a hobby, his young friend had learned ancient Aramaic and could read hieroglyphics. Young Ari also had his own theory on how ancient Egyptian was pronounced and sounded even though that dead language had not been spoken on earth for well over two thousand years! Mark soon realized that Ari matched Eric's intellect in many areas, but especially in his gift for multiple languages.

After his meeting was finished, Alexander ben Halevi popped his head into the room to say goodbye to both of them, then quickly left. After he departed, and during the course of their conversation, Mark discovered that Ari's other passion besides archeology was music. Ari explained that he was a composer and bandleader of his own band called "The Pistols", to which his father didn't approve. Mark also learned that Ari had a great sense of humor when Mark asked, "Why did you name your band "The Pistols"?

Grinning, Ari replied, "Because we can drink till midnight then piss till two!"

Mark chuckled loudly at this while saying, "I'm sorry I asked." However, at this point, Mark made a quick note to himself that this young man in front of him, in spite of his extraordinary metaphysical background, was still very unsteady about himself—even immature. Additionally, Mark discovered that Ari was single and loved chasing the ladies while being completely cool with the gay scene.

In fact, he invited both Eric and Mark to a club in Tel Aviv where his band was performing next Wednesday night about 9 p.m. to hear them. Before thinking to check with Eric to see if he was available, Mark readily agreed. Ari said that they should eat somewhere else first because the food at the club was really bad, but the booze and the music were great. He added that he would reserve them an excellent table. He also asked Mark if he liked American jazz. Mark replied, "I love jazz, but I haven't heard any in a long time."

Ari just said, "Well, then. Get ready, you're going to hear some Wednesday night. But now I have to go. See you Wednesday. I'll text you the directions to the club." Mark felt young again as he exchanged contact info with this comparative youngster—just like he used to do when meeting new people when he himself was much younger. He also very much enjoyed the youthful, high energy level of his new friend.

Back in the other room, after Alexander's departure, Jacob explained to Eric the impressive background of the man they had just met. They both agreed the meeting went well. Moreover, to make his point about Alexander, Jacob added, "Alexander said you will have his money for your campaign and whatever else you need. You have to remember when you speak to him that you are speaking to a man who controls the resources of a country. I believe he has his own personal army amongst other things at his disposal. You are now allied."

Eric thought for second. Most men would have been shaken at a statement like that. But all Eric said was, "Good, he could prove useful."

Lastly, before the meeting ended, and before Mark joined them, Eric added, "Jacob, I am sorry to ask again but I think Mark needs a top notch security guard assigned directly to him. The ones we have now are light weight. First, things can get dangerous on the campaign trail and I want him to be safe. But also we both know that Mark can take his projects to the legal limit. Sometimes even crossing it without knowing it. This could be embarrassing politically."

Before he went further, Jacob interrupted, "I know what you mean and I have the perfect person—Alisa Reichman, Sam's wife. I know he likes and respects her. She is not on any Mossad assignment right now. So I know she is available. I will have her given time off from her duties at the agency so as not to violate any campaign laws and you and Mark can pay her salary directly while on this assignment. After you win the election, the state will pay for the security for you both. I will set it up immediately." Mark then joined them and they both said goodbye to Jacob as they departed from his beautiful contemporary Jerusalem home.

Before Mark had a chance to tell Eric about their commitment on Wednesday night to hear Ari's band play, Eric's cell phone rang. It was Bo saying that Saul Jacoby had kept his word. The largest political party in Israel was holding a primary meeting tomorrow to select persons to be put on their party's list of candidates for Knesset seats in the upcoming election. Saul wanted Eric to attend to meet all the party's senior leadership and make sure he got on that list. Saul felt that because Eric was so well known and respected in Israel due to his military exploits, he would clinch the majority of seats necessary to form a new, one party government with Eric as Prime Minister and he as President of the Knesset. Eric's recent excellent publicity during the Maccabiah Games confirmed Saul's view that Eric was the strongest national candidate possible. Tomorrow he and Eric would convince the other senior party leaders to step aside and vigorously support Eric for PM. Saul strongly felt that Mark should attend as well. The meeting was set for after the Knesset, the Israeli Parliament, closed for business the next day at 5:30 p.m. at party headquarters.

While driving to the party meeting the next night, Eric turned to Mark saying, "I just thought of something that I am going to say in my speech tonight. I am sure to be asked if I support a two state solution. My answer is that we are going to buy a house and move to Samaria. I have found a nice house there. I ran across it years ago on a military mission. I know this comes as a surprise, but I hope it will lock in the settler vote."

Mark was stunned, saying, "But I love our present house. I don't want to move."

Eric replied, "You won't have to move. This is just a political statement. It is a way of generating votes. Trust me on this. But yes. We will buy the house." Mark was shaken but willing to follow Eric's lead.

At the political primary meeting at party headquarters, Bo Bergman made sure he was the first to arrive, followed by Eric and Mark. He greeted and introduced both of them personally to every senior party member that attended that night. Eric was very impressed with Bo's knowledge of the individual party members and their personal information. Eric soon realized that Bo was an extraordinary asset to his campaign, not only on the strategy level but on a grassroots level. Bo had a great deal of credibility with the senior party leadership and Eric felt that this credibility was rubbing off on him—helping him to be taken seriously as a candidate for prime minister. Saul Jacoby was doing his part too. He was working the room for Eric.

During Eric's speech that night, he announced that both he and Mark were moving to the West Bank as his response to the question about a two state solution. He said that his actions in the future will speak louder than words. The room burst into a standing ovation. As they were leaving the meeting, Bo approached Eric and whispered, "When you said you were moving to the West Bank, did you hear the giant sucking sound of all the settler political parties collapsing and folding into ours? I must say it is a brilliant political move and will generate lots of free publicity. Sorry I didn't think of it."

Eric spent the entire drive home calming Mark about this unexpected turn in their lives. By the time they arrived home, it was clear to both of them that they would buy the house but not physically move there. Mark put his foot down about the move. Mark's attitude reflected their age difference. Mark had disrupted his life by moving to Israel and marrying a partner much younger who still didn't mind, if not craved, adventure and a certain amount of disruption. Mark on the other hand, preferred a certain amount of stability. Of course, they both knew that Mark could deny Eric nothing if Eric really wanted it. The argument was settled when Eric explained that when he won the election, they would be spending most of their time living at the official residence of the prime minister in Jerusalem. Due to this, Eric argued, where their real home was wouldn't really matter. It was dawning on Mark that their lives were going to change in ways he had not foreseen, whether he wanted them to or not.

Getting out of the car, Mark finally remembered to tell Eric about their date the next night with Ari ben Halevi to hear his band. Eric stopped for a second to process this. Did he really want Mark getting close to that family? But he decided after a moment of indecision—that yes it was fine. So he replied, "I might be a little late if my political meeting runs late. But I will be there." Then he winked at Mark adding, "After all, I am not letting you go on a date with a good looking young guy all alone." Mark knew this was Eric's attempt at being funny. He always had such a strange sense of humor. But Mark was not amused by the inference that he would so easily cheat on his partner. However, he secretly enjoyed the fact that he aroused a certain amount of jealousy in Eric every now and then and was not above using Ari to do it.

When the party primary vote was held, Eric received the most votes in the party's history, setting him up to run for prime minister in the general election. Their intended move to Samaria (also called the West Bank) echoed beyond the primary vote, hitting the national press and positively affecting the upcoming election.

Mark was really looking forward to a night out in Tel Aviv. He hadn't been to a nightclub in ages. Since Eric was busy he decided to eat at a small local restaurant, sitting at the counter enjoying the comfort food it served. He didn't feel like cooking or being at home. This night was his night out. He arrived at the Tel Aviv nightclub early, around 8:30 p.m., feeling excited and a little giddy from the surrounding positive energy of the place. When he arrived, it was already packed with people. He was impressed with its young hip crowd. The stage was a foot (.3m) higher than the tables at ground level. Surrounding the ground level tables was a second tier of tables and chairs with a small metal fence separating the areas and two sets of steps on each side leading down to the ground level. Beyond that there was a long bar running along the wall on both sides of the room. There was already an act on stage playing the piano accompanied by a female singer with a beautiful voice. Mark entered and gave his name to the maître d' and was led by a waiter to his reserved table next to the stage. As promised by Ari, most would consider it the best table in the house. He ordered a vodka on the rocks and began to listen to the female singer's beautiful voice singing a song about love. Mark really started to enjoy the music, almost swaying to it with the enthusiastic crowd.

While surveying the bar he noticed a familiar face. It was Alisa Reichman just arriving at the bar. She recognized him too. He immediately motioned for her to join him which she did. As she sat at the table, he said, "Good to see a familiar face. I didn't know you liked clubs like this."

She replied, "Oh yes. I get around." Alisa Riechman was one of Mossad's most lethal agents with the code name The Viper reflecting her lightening moves against an enemy. A former yoga instructor and gymnast, she was also a mother of three sons—soon to be a grandmother but still in fighting form—and married to Sam Reichman. Sam Reichman was now the chief of Mossad and was a good friend of Eric's. He had also joined Eric on many of Mossad's most dangerous missions. Alisa had known and liked both Eric and Mark before they had gotten married. So on this assignment to protect Mark she felt more like a mother hen than a lethal spy.

Mark asked what she was drinking, and she replied, "Just a diet coke, please." Mark called over the waiter to take the order but before the waiter left, Eric also arrived, ordered a whisky straight up, said hello to Alisa and joined them. Mark noticed he didn't seem surprised to see her. Alisa now confessed to Mark that it was no accident that she met him here at the club. She was his new personal bodyguard. Mark responded with a knowing smile, "At least they picked someone I like." They didn't have time for any more small talk.

As Eric sat at the table, his face was so well known that the audience all turned to look at him. So much so that the singer stopped her show to announce that they had a celebrity in the house tonight, calling him by name and announcing he was running for Prime Minister. Eric stood up to wave at the audience and thank them before sitting down and motioning the singer to please carry on with her performance. She had to wait until the applause for him stopped. Mark looked straight at Eric when he was seated, saying, "You have a knack for good publicity. Don't you?" Just then the waiter brought the drinks. So, they all raised their glasses saying "L'chaim!" which is a Hebrew toast meaning "To Life."

Afterwards, Eric responded, "Just to clarify, I am here to meet our new friend because he invited us and you committed us. I hope he comes on soon because I have an 8 a.m. campaign meeting tomorrow."

While Eric was talking, Mark couldn't help but notice the intensity of the looks by the ladies in the audience at Eric—as if they could devour him. Trying to keep a cool head, Mark thought to himself, *Now look who's jealous after all these years. It's the curse of having a movie star handsome partner. I'm just going to ignore it as usual.* He also knew by now that although his husband did a good job at pretending to ignore the attention, Eric was acutely aware of it and enjoyed the adoration.

The excellent female singer finished her performance to a standing ovation from the audience. Next came the jazz band called The Pistols. It consisted of a piano player, a bass player, a trumpet player and a drummer. To Mark's surprise, not only did Ari play the trumpet in the band, but he played it extremely well. In fact, Mark thought that Ari was the best he had ever heard, including the famous trumpet player Louis Armstrong. Ari's trumpet playing was almost hypnotizing in its beauty and power. The audience was mesmerized by it too. After a forty five minute music set—somewhat long by music standards—there was dead silence from the audience for a minute when Ari finished. When the audience caught its breath, it went wild with a standing ovation. Both Alisa and Eric felt the power of Ari's trumpet playing too. They all looked at each other with same question on their faces, "Who is this guy, Ari, we're meeting here?"

They didn't have to wait long for Ari to come out and join them at their table. He shook hands with both Alisa and Eric who he had not previously met. Mark thought he noticed a quick almost imperceptible sense of tension or even defiance in Ari's eyes as he shook Eric's hand but said nothing, dismissing his observation as nonsense. Or, Mark thought to himself, maybe Ari was just nervous about meeting someone who could become the country's next Prime Minister. Still Mark remembered what he felt when he shook Ari's hand and wondered if Ari had felt something when he shook Eric's. Coincidently, he also noticed that from the moment Ari shook Eric's hand, Ari never took his eyes off Eric. It wasn't a look of adulation but a look like when a hunter finally focuses on its prey in the forest.

In any case, they all told Ari how impressed they were with his music. He, of course, politely said thank you. Ari mentioned that he composed the jazz performance he just played. Out of the blue, Eric challenged him saying, "You know what this country lacks? It's a good military marching song for the troops. I think it's time we got one. If you're so good, write one for us."

Ari, somewhat surprised by this request, accepted the challenge, saying "Give me your napkin and I will write the lyrics now." With that, on the back of the napkin he wrote the following musical refrain and gave it to Eric:

"From Mount Hermon to the Seas
This land belongs to me!
ISSIS be damned!
This here is Israel's land!
By God's Will we stand!"

Ari ended by saying, "I will send Mark the musical score tomorrow. Since you probably can't read music. Just show it to your marching band leader. He'll play it for you. But do you like the lyrics?"

Eric read the lyrics aloud to everyone. Then said, "I love them. Now let's see what you can do with the tune. Do you want the napkin back?"

Ari replied, "Not necessary. The lyrics are permanently in my head. I will also give you the Hebrew version on the final score."

During the light banter of the next twenty minutes or so, Eric mentioned that he thought Ari's main passion was archeology. Ari replied that yes, it was. Mark interjected that he had never visited the tunnels underneath the prayer plaza by the Western Wall and on a hunch, asked Ari if he would like to go together someday. Ari instantly said, "I love those tunnels. I know them well. Why don't you let me be your guide and show them to you?"

Mark replied, "Agreed. But I am busy with Eric's campaign now. The tour will have to wait a while, but I will call you to set it up. I promise." The evening ended on a happy note with Mark promising to follow up with Ari and Eric saying he needed to leave to get up early for a meeting the next day. Eric, Mark and Alisa left the bar at the same time to go home. Ari stayed to play his next set but was quick to notice that a dozen plain clothed security guards got up from the audience and left the bar at the same time as his friends. Ari could recognize security guards almost immediately because his father traveled with so many. He guessed it was how they dressed that always alerted him.

As he watched his new friends depart through the crowded club, he also could not shake the feeling that Eric was not the right leader for Israel. *But who am I,* he thought, *to question the fitness of the most popular war hero in the country to be the next Prime Minister?* Nevertheless, Ari could not forget the utter blackness encasing outright evil he had seen in Eric when he shook his hand. Ordinarily he would ask his new friend Mark who he felt to be an astute old soul for help. But Ari also understood that on this issue Mark was blinded by love for Eric. Ari would have to try to get Mark to see the light about Eric or try to fix this himself. And his father wouldn't be any help either. His father was blinded by his business interests. As soon as his father asked him not to discuss the meeting at Jacob Kurtz's house with anyone, Ari assumed that some sort of deal had been struck between his father and Eric. And Ari knew his father did not tolerate any interference in his deals. However, something in Ari allowed him to see the evil in Eric. He deeply felt that God did not approve of Eric to lead Israel. Before he began his next music set, he somehow understood that Eric and he were mortal enemies. And he must and will do anything to stop him.

Ari had no idea that he only had one ally and guide in what would become his quest to save the people of Israel and the world from the horror that was about to engulf them, and that was the Lord God Himself. From the moment he had touched Eric, God had filled Ari with the strength of his spiritual power. After many millennia God had chosen a direct descendent of His hereditary priesthood for the upcoming fight against evil. Ari's life was already changing. Instead of chasing the ladies after his performance, he had an overwhelming urge to go back to his small bachelor apartment to study the Hebrew Bible and Talmud, which he did. It was the first of many days studying the religious holy books. In spite of this, Ari still felt uncertain about himself and his own belief in God. He had not yet realized his journey to find his faith in God had begun to prepare him for what was to come.

CHAPTER SIX

WAR BY OTHER MEANS

To paraphrase the famous quote by Prussian General, Carl von Clausewitz, "Politics is war by other means." And retired Colonel Eric Jansen proved a master at it with the help of his political strategist, Bo Bergman. They were an unbeatable team. The next 45 days until the general election was a constant flurry of speeches, meetings, podcasts and kissing the babies of adoring fans. They campaigned as much online as they did in person. Mark also carried his weight campaigning with Eric. They both walked in the Gay Pride Parade. They maxed their free TV ad time given to all candidates by the government. They were very strict about only accepting the maximum political contributions allowed by law. In fact, Eric Jansen campaigned for prime minister with the promise of complete transparency from the government. No major changes to government institutions would be made or tolerated—moderation in all forms was Eric's outward policy. And no, he was not for the two state solution. He was the first major candidate to say this. They also went to their friend Rabbi Itshak Sofer, the one who they saved from being robbed, and convinced him to tell his followers that if they wouldn't vote for an openly gay man, then they shouldn't vote at all. This had the effect of lessening the ultra-orthodox vote count, thus further assuring Eric's victory. In return, they cut a financial deal with Rabbi Sofer that included an increase of state funds for the ultra-orthodox schools where his followers studied while the other ultra-orthodox school funding would be frozen. All these maneuverings had their desired effect on national election day when Eric's party received a majority in the Knesset parliament, securing 73 seats out of 121. Eric swept into office as the leader of the majority party with no need to compromise or form a coalition—as planned!

The bad news was that both Eric and Mark were exhausted after this campaign. And even worse, during Eric's swearing-in ceremony, a barrage of missiles from both Hamas in the Gaza strip in the South and Hezbollah from Lebanon in the North was launched against Israel. They were sending a message of their disapproval of Eric's election. The new Prime Minister immediately directed the Israeli High Command to return fire but keep it limited—tit for tat so to speak—while shooting down all missiles and protecting Israeli civilian population centers. This displayed a moderate first reaction to a provocation.

In the meantime, Eric listened to Bo Bergman's advice to pick technocrats and government professionals with major experience in their respective fields to staff his cabinet and government departments. Eric also fulfilled his promise to Saul Jacoby, making him President of the Knesset. Eric soon discovered that Saul was an excellent choice since he was extremely effective in managing the Knesset. All these outwardly excellent appointments of moderates made Israel look much more appealing to the global financial markets and foreign allies such as the United States and Europe. The collective West loved him. His first press conference at the end of his first day as Prime Minister was balanced but firm, discussing his response to the new missile attacks and promising safety to his fellow Israelis. Publicly, he was the epitome of diplomacy and strength—a vision of a steel fist in a velvet glove. He also announced the discovery of a major copper deposit in the Negev desert and government plans for a transparent bidding process to develop it into major copper mine, making Israel a player in the global mining industry. No one guessed that this man they had just elected had two personalities with two quite different agendas!

The next day, Eric rose early with the part of him Mark called Eric's black side in complete control, to be driven in the prime minister limousine surrounded by a military motorcade to Technicon University. The university is in Haifa and is equivalent to MIT in the United States. He was there for an unannounced meeting with the two pilots who had flown Dragon Fire, the laser armed aerial battleship, into battle on his last covert mission. Currently, the two pilots were both senior professors at the university, holding doctorate degrees in robotics and biophysics as applied to advanced military technological warfare. Gil Sofer was a widower with no children, ten years older than Elon Dagen. Elon had never married and had maintained his thin muscled figure, which made him look somewhat gaunt now that he was older. Both men were fanatically devoted to their country and to the pursuit of science.

Colonel Gil Sofer and Captain Elon Dagen recognized Eric instantly as he walked outside of their glass-walled offices. They got up from their desks, opened their doors, and greeted him warmly. Colonel Gil Sofer was the first to speak, saying, "Congratulations on winning the election. Elon and I both voted for you. And welcome. I thought we would get a visit from you. We've been preparing for it."

All Eric said was, "I'm furious."

Captain Elon Dagen interrupted him immediately saying, "We need to speak in the secure room which is just around the corner. Follow me."

Three minutes later they were all seated in a secure conference room. It was a room with no windows and only one door. The walls, floor and ceiling were double lined with lead to completely shield anyone in the room from any electronic monitoring device. There were two old style phones on the table to make or receive phone calls. No cell phones would work. There was also a large television screen on the wall at one end of the room. Col. Gil Sofer spoke first, saying, "I ordered some coffee and Danish pastries for us from my cellphone before we got in here. It should arrive very soon." Eric, somewhat surprised at this offer, thought this was needlessly polite but didn't say anything.

Eric Jansen immediately started explaining why he was there. "Fucking Hamas and fucking Hezbollah tried to embarrass me at my swearing in ceremony. They wanted to send me a message. Well, I got it and I want to send one back to them. One that they will never forget. In fact a message so strong that it will end this conflict once and for all. I remembered that the laser weapon on Dragon Fire was able to incinerate 200 terrorists in Central Africa in minutes— zapped to death—leaving nothing behind but a bit of smoke. So I want to know the status of that program and if it can be used to solve our terrorist problem closer to home? And if so, why haven't you used it before?" Both Gil and Elon looked at each with a slight smile. They could tell the new prime minister was dead serious. And they were ready for the question with an answer.

But before they could answer, an almost seven foot (30 cm) tall humanoid-like robot with a shiny gray outer skin entered the room. He was introduced by Colonel Sofer as Joshua and was pushing a cart with hot coffee and pastries. His face looked like a mask with his eyes, mouth and nose rudimentarily sculpted on it. His eyeballs, though, glowed with white lights through horizontal slits. He stopped the conversation cold when he asked Eric in perfectly clear Hebrew how he took his coffee, and if he would like milk or sugar. He spoke without moving his lips, for he had no lips to move. The Joshua's voice was masculine with a very slight metallic sound to it. Eric was stunned as the Joshua stood by his side waiting for direction. Colonel Gil Sofer quickly said, "Joshua, speak English to the Prime Minister."

The robot Joshua repeated his coffee preparation request in perfectly clear English. Finally, recovering from the shock of this Frankenstein looking robot calmly standing so close to him, Eric said in a command like tone, "I take my coffee black." With that, Joshua poured a perfectly filled—to a half inch (1.3cm) below the brim—paper cup of hot black coffee from a plastic pitcher and gently placed it in front of Eric.

Joshua then added, "I also have prune, apple or strawberry Danish pastries. Which would you like?" When Eric did not respond quickly enough, Joshua added, "To clarify, I meant to say French pastries instead of Danish." Eric replied that he would try the strawberry. Again, Joshua gently and perfectly placed the pastry in front of him on a small plate. He repeated this process for each of them. Eric was intensely focused on each little movement and sound the humanoid-like robot made. It moved with the smoothness and dexterity of an athlete, no clunks or thuds that one would expect from something that size. Eric was transfixed. After Joshua finished serving, it stood waiting for further orders, asking Colonel Sofer, "Does the Creator wish anything else?"

Col. Sofer replied, "Nothing else for now."

With that, the Joshua said, "It was pleasure serving you gentlemen." He then left the room, gently closing the door behind him.

Elon Dagen was looking directly at Eric with one raised eyebrow. "Yes. Yes. I know. He's a great waiter. But he cleans even better," Elon said. "We've eliminated our nightly housekeeping staff here. And his cooking is superb. He makes the best caesar salad you've ever tasted. We named him after the Jewish general in the Bible who conquered Canaan. We have also programmed him to speak twelve languages perfectly. But I know what you really want to discuss. Under battle test training conditions, he is the perfect soldier. He is almost indestructible, he follows orders perfectly and is a killing machine with the strength of a dozen men. He is fearless and relentless. We programed him to understand and use all military weapons systems, from knives to the most sophisticated electronic weapons. But I have to warn you that at this point, he has not been tested under real battlefield conditions. Moreover, the main reason the program was shut down was because of Joshua's lack of morality. He cannot judge right from wrong and will kill anything and everything in front of him in battle. Joshua cannot distinguish between enemy combat soldiers and non-combatant women and children. The former Prime Minister shut our entire program down because of it. He said it was a question of morality." Elon Dagen stopped to take a breath and see if Eric was fully understanding what he had just been told. Then, adding a touch of sarcasm, he continued, "Sorry you were interrupted when Joshua entered. You were saying something about giving our enemies a lesson they would never forget?"

Eric thought he had seen it all, but this was something completely new to him. He sat for several minutes saying nothing, processing what he had just witnessed. The other two men understood his silent reaction. What they could not tell about their new prime minister was Eric's elation swelling inside of him. Eric thought to himself, *I want an army of these things and the aerial battleships too!* Finally, Eric said, "Who knows something like this exists, and who can give it orders?"

Colonel Sofer answered, "Now six people including yourself know about Joshua. And no foreign country knows about our robotic developments either. He will only follow verbal orders from Captain Dagen or myself. But for more complicated directions such as military action, you have to know the codes to activate him. And we are the only two people who know the codes. However, in our next upgrade we will eliminate the necessity of the attack codes. All directions will then be by verbal command."

Eric lowered his voice and said in his most serious, even deadly, tone, "I am looking for men who will do what needs to be done regardless of the circumstances. Who will follow my orders without question. I am looking for people who want to change the reality of the Middle East to secure the State of Israel." To make his point further, he added, "I am not looking to take a lot of prisoners. In fact, my philosophy in battle will be to take no prisoners at all. Israel Defense Forces will not follow such orders. Can I count on you both? Are you with me? Also, I want you to program them to follow my orders. I want them to consider me their creator as well." Yes, Eric Jansen understood exactly what he had just been told about the lack of moral judgement in his future robot soldiers. Looking straight at Eric without blinking, both men told him they were definitely with him and agreed with him.

Both Colonel Sofer and Captain Dagen started to relax when they understood that their new PM was there to expand their robot project, not shut it down. The remaining tension in the room dissipated completely when Eric said, "I am glad to hear that you are with me. From what I have just seen, I believe Israel has a massive technological military advantage. We just have to use it correctly. So how many of these robots have you built and how many more aerial battle ships like Dragon Fire are under construction?"

In reply, Colonel Sofer said, "So far, Joshua is the only one of his kind. The previous administration shut down all our funding after we returned with you from Africa because of the morality question. It deeply disturbed him that we incinerated 200 plus terrorists. So nothing else has been done on the Dragon Fire program either. We have just the one aerial battleship ready, as you know since we have all previously flown in it together. Additionally, we were only able to finish building one Joshua robot by diverting funds from other programs. The good news is that very few people know about this robot program because it has never been specifically funded."

"I will get you all the funding you need," Eric said. "And I will have it for you quickly. It won't be government funding but from a private source. But I need to know from you the approximate costs. Also I have decided to promote you, Colonel Sofer, to Brigadier General in charge of military robotics and our space program. Captain Dagen for your immense contribution to our military defenses I am promoting you to Full Colonel, skipping two ranks. I will make these recommendations to the IDF General Staff tomorrow. How long will it take to make more Joshua units? And I want at least six more aerial battleships. I believe these robots and aerial battleships will give us overwhelming ground and air superiority. These robots mean that potentially no Israeli soldier has to die for safeguarding the State of Israel."

Both Gil Sofer and Elon Dagen were positively beaming at their prime minister for giving them military promotions. While they loved their teaching roles at the university, the promotions from Eric justified their life's work. At heart they were both scientists first and last. Both men now sat forward in their seats around the conference table facing Eric. Their body language reflected the seriousness of what they were about to discuss. Captain Elon Dagen spoke first, saying, "The production of the first Joshua unit was very costly at about $400 million. Its brain that I built with advanced artificial intelligence was the part that was the most expensive and longest in development. Its brain is unique. It consists of a secret liquid formula with floating neutrino particles that opened a door to a new level of physics powered by electricity that I alone understand. To simplify it for you, each electrical impulse is a bit of information that can be stored in the liquid of the robot brain. Its brain has the capacity to store billions of bits of information riding on electricity. Thus, in theory, Joshua could become sentient or self-aware one day. But for now, Joshua has the ability to self-learn which it does extremely quickly. Therefore, Joshua itself will construct the next units. In turn, the new robots will build more units. So I believe the time it takes to make each robot and cost per unit should drop dramatically to about $1 million each or less as we scale up."

"I was the one who developed the original aerial battleship which we named Dragon Fire," Gil added. "Its cost to build was just under one billion dollars. The most expensive part to develop was the antigravity fusion engine that powers it. Elon and I jointly developed the laser weapon technology. But in the future those costs should also drop dramatically because we can use the Joshua units to construct more battleships and laser weapons. In fact, we can use the Joshuas to fly them.

This will make space travel almost immediately possible since our holdup was bringing earth atmosphere into space for human pilots. We will be able to control the fleet from a control center on the ground. I cannot give you a cost figure yet for the aerial battleships. But I can tell you that the cost will be dramatically less. However, at first, I foresee the need to divert some of the Joshua units from soldiers to engineers, construction workers, and pilots to make it happen."

Eric to make sure what he just heard, asked, "Gil, I thought you said when we were flying at Mach 3 during our last mission that Dragon Fire could achieve Mach 6 speed fast enough to leave earth orbit but had never been tested at those speeds. So if we don't have to worry about humans surviving at those speeds or in a zero oxygen atmosphere, then could we use Joshua robot units to fly the battleships into space and mine minerals from the moon? Then no Israeli would have to die. And we could do this relatively quickly?"

"Yes!" Gil and Elon exclaimed simultaneously. Eric couldn't help but smile when he heard that answer.

Lastly, Elon Dagen added, "We will not need any expensive semiconductors or other electric parts. The robot brain is all liquid with impulses generated by neutrino electrical reactions running through it. Since I invented the way for these impulses to be transmitted and stored, they now have memory and can learn things and solve problems. My theory is that since the robots can now learn and solve problems faster, they will be able to build smarter and smarter robots and in turn better and better soldiers. I will personally supervise this part of their production very closely." By this time, it was obvious to Eric that there was an intense rivalry between the two men. He came to the conclusion that even though they worked together, they really didn't like each other.

"Before I leave here today, make me a Creator like you so I am able to command Joshua," Eric insisted.

With that request, Elon Dagen opened the door and asked the Joshua robot, who had been waiting outside, to enter. As the Joshua stood by Eric Jansen, Elon Dagen said, "Joshua I am your Creator and I command you to acknowledge Eric Jansen, the man in front of you, as your Creator also." Elon then turned to Eric Jansen and said, "Speak to the Joshua so he can recognize your voice."

Eric then said, "I am Eric Jansen, Prime Minister of Israel. Do you acknowledge me as your Creator?"

The Joshua responded, "Creator, what is your command?"

"It's done," Elon said. "He recognizes you as a Creator. You can now command him."

Eric had one more question. "Do the Joshuas have any weaknesses? You said they were almost indestructible."

Elon responded, "Only one. If he lost electric power by being grounded. So I put thick rubber sole pads on his feet to prevent that from happening. Additionally, we think that he is so tightly made that normal rainfall or water emersion will have no effect on his internal electrical charge. But this has yet to be fully tested."

Gil Sofer was sensing that the meeting was coming to an end, but had to tell Eric one more thing. "Just for your consideration, before our program was shut down we were about to miniaturize the laser weapon on Dragon Fire to be used as a handgun. We were at the last stages of miniaturization. I think we should continue this vein of development."

Eric was surprised by yet another new military weapon advancement. He tried to make light of his surprise, saying, "If you mean you were in the process of developing a ray gun? I love the idea and will approve the funding for further development and testing. But now I need to leave. I will be speaking with you both again soon. One more thing for the record, if you are ever asked what transpired at this meeting, say I visited only to congratulate you personally on your new promotions. Everything else is highly classified." As Eric stood to leave, he took one last look directly at both men. "Also for the record, as Prime Minister, I now officially authorize you both to develop a robot army for the State of Israel. The name for this secret program will be the Joshua Project." Both Gil Sofer and Elon Dagen nodded their heads in full agreement.

As Eric settled into the backseat of the government provided, chauffeured limousine, he felt very satisfied and smiled to himself. The bottom line was that he needed those two men to achieve his future military goals and he had just bought their loyalty or at least their full cooperation. He felt that they worshipped science for its own sake which could prove useful in achieving his goals. He also realized that he could use the intense competition between these two men to his advantage. No one in the world realized his true goal of developing a killer robot army that was not subject to any moral constraints, directly loyal to him, and based on his own long hidden, personal belief of kill or be killed.

Gil Sofer and Elon Dagen did not know it then, but they had just made a massive miscalculation by giving creator status to Eric Jansen. Not them or anybody else in the world, with the exception of Ari ben Halevi, recognized who Eric Jansen actually was. The problem with Eric Jansen was that he had spent a lifetime hiding his killer side, albeit currently kept under control by a loving relationship with his partner. Added to this was recurring uncontrolled episodes of PTSD caused by his very hazardous service in the military and now the extra stress due to his growing anxiety over possible betrayal while exercising power as prime minister. This was a position he was determined to never give up. All this meant that a full-blown sociopath was now leading the country, unable to determine right from wrong and willing to do anything to protect his country and hang on to power. Furthermore, as a sociopath, he was a master manipulator able to hide his true feelings and plans from everyone, including his partner and closest friends.

After the meeting it was almost 10 a.m. and Eric Jansen needed to get to his new prime minister's office pronto to start his day. He knew he would have dozens of items on his desk that needed his attention. On the way back in his limo, he made a cellphone call to Alexander ben Halevi asking him if they could meet to discuss the funding and construction of a new top secret military defense project. The two men agreed to meet early the next morning in the prime minister's office. It would take place in the PM's secure conference room. After his call, Eric passed a crowd of his adoring supporters. He stopped, got out of the limo, waved to the crowd and held up and kissed a baby so the crowd could snap photos before continuing on his way. His timing was perfect and public image was golden!

The next morning at 7 a.m., before most people arrived in the Prime Minister's office, Alexander ben Halevi took a seat across from Eric in the secure conference room. After good morning pleasantries between the two, Eric got up to serve them both some coffee. While doing this, Eric thought to himself that Alexander would never guess in a hundred years who or rather what had served him coffee yesterday. He got right down to business by saying, "Alex, I am going to develop a top secret military defense project that will give Israel a decisive technological advantage in our next war. And I need your financial help. Unfortunately, I can't use public funding or tell you what it is at this time."

"I am all about helping Israel, but I need to make money as well," Alexander responded.

"I need a billion dollars for its development," Eric explained. "With another billion dollars as a backup if needed. I predict that in less than two years you will be able to triple, if not quadruple, your money by selling this system to select allies. Especially once the world sees this system in action. You will have the exclusive sale rights to a unique military defense system and its production. I have done my research on you too. I know you are already heavily invested in defense and armament companies around the world, so this would be a perfect fit for you. However, this is very top secret therefore I cannot fund it through government sources. In fact, I want you to split up the production so that no one company or division of yours can tell what the finished project will be. I am sure we can find more than a dozen sites to produce this. One more point is that I want it all produced and developed in Israel."

Alexander took his time processing what Eric had just proposed before he replied, "Eric, you offer me no guarantees except your word that this defense system will be profitable or even functional. I need to take it on your word. So, I will make available to you the two billion dollars for this project on one condition. In addition to the exclusive rights to produce and sell this system beyond Israel, I may or may never come to you one day and ask you for a favor. If I do ask, it's a favor you cannot and will not refuse. This is what I want."

Eric also took his time before replying. He hadn't anticipated such an open ended commitment to Alexander. The favor could be anything. Even a request to kill or have someone killed. On the other hand, he thought to himself, killing had never been a problem for him. So after just a minute to think about it, he said, "Agreed. Brigadier General Gil Sofer will be your contact on the project."

"Then we have a deal," Alexander said happily. "Your General's contact on this project will be the head of my defense division. I will inform him today. Your funds will be ready to be drawn upon from an account in the Cayman Islands tomorrow morning." The meeting ended on friendly terms. To draw less attention to himself, Alexander ben Halevi departed the way he arrived, through the back way of the prime minister's office complex.

CHAPTER SEVEN

.ᐠᘏᓂᐟ.

BALFOUR HOUSE

Moving a household puts stress on all relationships and Eric and Mark were no different in this respect. Because of the extreme difference in their schedules due to the political campaign, they had not slept in the same bed together for the previous two months. They had mutually agreed it would be easier to sleep in separate bedrooms, so as not to disturb each other. Mark initially joked that they were experiencing the seven year itch syndrome a little early. Their interests had always been separate, but seemed to be growing even further apart. Eric thrived on the prestige, limelight and especially the power of being prime minister, whereas Mark was growing more unhappy with his life. He particularly did not like the loss of privacy. Mark felt that everything revolved around Eric while he was just an observer. The upcoming household move only added to their relationship tension. Mark's frustration was that he was still very much in love with his partner. He just did not know yet how to draw a balance between their relationship and Eric's new job as PM.

Luckily for them, they agreed to look at the prime minister's residence called Balfour House before they actually moved there. It was a historically significant building, the site of many meetings of famous people intertwined with the founding of the State of Israel, located dead center in the new part of Jerusalem. The name Balfour House is famous throughout Israel. But it was obvious to Mark that it had not been properly maintained. It was a mishmash of architectural styles, too small for their needs and the last renovation had been stopped midway from completion. The only thing that Mark felt it had going for it was its location. It was in a beautiful upscale residential neighborhood. Indeed, the semi-attached prime minister's office was also very close to the residence. That made high security easier to achieve since it could be concentrated in one area. As they walked over construction debris from the unfinished renovation, Mark turned to Eric and said, "This place is unlivable and I refuse to live here. And for the record the prime minister's office building looks like something from a bad 1930's prison movie."

In response, Eric made a split second decision, knowing this could be a major issue in their relationship as well as affecting his job. So he simply said, as earnestly as possible,

"I agree with you." Their homes—where they lived and how they were decorated—had always been Mark's jurisdiction. Eric has no taste and no interest in modern architecture or interior design, so he took other people's word that Mark had excellent taste. But Eric was an old hand in negotiating with Mark and knew he had recently neglected his partner, so he added, "In fact, would you like to take over the project of developing a new governmental complex? I know you have an eye for that sort of thing. I believe several plans have been authorized and funded but then stopped. The country needs someone to review the plans and carry them to fruition."

A big smile came over Mark's face. Mark was thrilled, as he replied, "I love the idea of contributing. Does this mean I can assemble a team of architects and interior designers?"

"Yes," Eric replied. "I said it's all been funded. But good luck finding a plot big enough to accommodate it all in Jerusalem."

Unfortunately for Mark they were not alone—the prime minister's security detail was all around them. Otherwise Mark would have embraced his big blond hunk of a husband on the spot. Eric read the vibes in his partner and said, "Yes, I know it's been too long. But tonight for sure I will be home early. And in the meantime, until our new residence is ready, we will live in our current home." As they departed Balfour

House, Mark already knew that he was up to the challenge. The only thing he would keep of this old place was the name, while the new place would be designed by Israeli architects and have art by Israeli artists hanging on its walls promoting Israeli culture. And as for a plot of land big enough for this project, he remembered reading in the newspapers about a couple of religious institutions sitting on big parcels of land who disliked their current location in Jerusalem because the new city had grown up around them. They might be very interested in a land swap and the opportunity to move to this tranquil, leafy green, residential neighborhood. He was also sure that the neighbors of the current Balfour House would love to see the current double and triple security barricades on the streets surrounding it gone from their neighborhood.

Indeed, Eric came home early that night. In anticipation, Mark had prepared his favorite dinner of paprika chicken with his favorite side dishes and strawberry short cake for dessert. They made love that night for the first time in a long time. Afterwards, they both agreed that make up sex can be extraordinarily fun. As they lay in bed together, Eric was especially relaxed and pleased with himself. His political popularity in the country had never been higher. For the moment Israel's borders were quiet. He had also strengthened Israel's important foreign alliances. Moreover, his carefully planned image of the moderate who united the country had held. Recently he had been updated by General Sofer that the Joshua robots were duplicating themselves on the production lines at a faster rate than they had estimated. General Sofer had also reorganized and centralized the robot and battleship production into one secret facility in the Negev desert. They were more than doubling their numbers every week and the newer ones seemed to be more lethal! Apparently, robots making robots fixed flaws that humans missed. Soon he would have his first battalion of soldier robots to deploy. Additionally, no one had yet noticed that he had already replaced his own security detail with soldiers from his former Special Forces unit who are personally loyal to him. He had almost done the same with key positions in the Israeli Defense Forces and Shin Bet (police). This was done slowly and methodically but steadily, making no waves and backing off when necessary.

Eric was feeling secure and relaxed. So, when Mark suddenly got the idea into his head that Ari's band should play at Jacob and Miriam's upcoming wedding and asked if Eric would be bothered by him making this recommendation, Eric didn't seem to care. Half asleep, he said, "It wouldn't bother me in the least. Do whatever you want." They then fell asleep in each other's arms.

The next day Mark called Eric's mother, Miriam Jansen, to see if she and Jacob Kurtz had chosen a band for their wedding yet. They had not. So he highly recommended Ari's band. He told her that she and Jacob could catch the band every Wednesday night playing jazz at a club in Tel Aviv. But he added that he thought they could play any kind of music they wanted for the wedding. She thought they could make it to see them next Wednesday night. So, he told her he would call Ari to make sure they got a good table for the show. Miriam also told him that they had finally picked the date for the wedding. It was going to be six weeks from today and that he and Eric were the first to know. She said they don't want any wedding presents but instead would pick two charities for guests to donate to if they wished. Of course, Mark said, "Mazel tov! We're definitely coming. I'll tell Eric."

He then called Ari to tell him who was coming to see his show and that they might have a wedding gig for his band. Ari was delighted to hear the news. "I'll take care of them," he said. "And I just want you to know that I make my money this way. I don't take a shekel from my father. So thank you for the referral." This financial revelation somehow didn't surprise Mark. Ari then continued, "So when are you going to let me be your guide to the tunnels under Jerusalem?" This question took Mark by surprise. Because of his overwhelming involvement in Eric's political campaign, he had forgotten about his own interests such as the tunnel system under Jerusalem and the strange, almost ethereal, sound of a trumpet or horn coming from it.

Mark answered Ari's question with a question. "Yes, what about meeting tomorrow at the prayer plaza in front of the Western Wall? If you're available?" They agreed to meet after lunch at 1p.m. to start their tour and spend a fun day exploring the remains of the ancient underground caverns of Jerusalem. Little did they know what they would discover!

CHAPTER EIGHT

THE WESTERN WALL HERITAGE FOUNDATION

"It is forbidden to step one foot under the actual Temple Mount. We don't want to start a holy war. That is why all our extensive excavations go under the existing old city or along the outer supporting wall of the Temple Mount, but none of our explorations go under the Temple itself! Period—Full Stop!" That is what the tour guide announced as he started the tour for Ari and Mark, along with six other tourists and Alisa Reichman who accompanied them for security but also to keep these two from getting into trouble. And for some reason she felt her motherly instinct to keep them away from trouble was flashing red today.

Just before the tour started, when Alisa was at a discreet enough distance away that she would not be able to hear their conversation, Mark confessed a secret to Ari. In a low voice, almost a whisper, Mark said, "I know this sounds crazy, but when I prayed at the Western Wall I heard a trumpet or horn playing. And as far as I could understand, no one else heard it. I thought the sound was coming from under the ground."

Ari, staring directly back at Mark responded, "I've heard the trumpet too in the underground tunnels we are about to see. I tried to find where the sound was coming from but couldn't. Maybe we can search for it today if we hear it?" Both men then fell silent, a little surprised that the other had also heard it.

Seeing Alisa walk closer within hearing distance, Ari immediately switched to a louder and more assured tone. He displayed a level of knowledge about the underground city that was equal to any guide. "Let me explain what you both are about to see," he said to Mark and Alisa. "Digging deep pits and tunnels under Jerusalem started in the mid nineteenth century by Westerners, who in many cases were more adventurers or religious zealots than archeologists. In most cases, this well meaning but haphazard process of discovering what was under the Holy City continued until the State of Israel conquered the Old City of Jerusalem in 1967. Then, The Western Wall Heritage Foundation and Israeli Antiquities Authority took control of all archeological work in and under the city. The Palestinians opposed all underground tunnel exploration because they believed that such archeological explorations would be used as a tool of western imperialism and the Jews to undermine the Islamic presence in Al-Quds and in the Harem al-Sharif. These are the Islamic names for Jerusalem and the Temple Mount where the Al-Aqsa Mosque sits. This mosque currently sits on top of the traditional site of the Jewish Holy Temple which was destroyed by the ancient Roman army. I won't go into the theories of where the actual Holy Temple stood, but suffice it to say that the actual historical site where the Temple stood compared to where the Al-Aqsa Mosque stands today is controversial amongst non-Moslem scholars."

Five minutes later, the tour started at the official entrance to the underground tunnels close to the Western Wall. They all descended stone steps for about 50 feet (15m) from street level and entered the underground world of ancient Jerusalem. They progressed through well lit passages and newly dug tunnels held in place by massive steel girders which reinforced the towering ceiling. The tour covered all sorts of interesting places such as an ancient Roman amphitheater cut into the solid rock side of the Temple Mount; a huge banquet hall covered in faded frescos that the guide theorized was probably used by King Herod the Great and his descendants for royal banquets entertaining visiting dignitaries; and a medieval church and ancient cisterns connected by a maze of ancient water channels cut into solid rock. Although the roof was held in place by strong steel beams, everyone on the tour couldn't shake a nervous feeling brought on by the vibrations of the bustling streets and houses of Jerusalem over their heads. The vibrations made it feel like everything could collapse at any moment, bringing the entire city—buildings and streets—crashing down on their heads.

However, the tour proceeded uneventfully until they came to a narrow passage which is called the Western Wall Tunnel. It runs directly alongside the entire Western Wall bedrock foundation and exits at the north end of the Temple Mount. Now that the tunnel is completely open at both ends, a nice breeze blows through it. When the north end of the tunnel was first opened by explosives, blowing away the debris of centuries, the city Moslems rioted for weeks. But they soon realized that no harm was done to the Temple Mount and that the tunnel brought tourists to the city who would spend their money in local stores. Currently, the north end of the tunnel is sometimes open to tourists and sometimes closed due to security concerns. Inside the tunnel, on the wall of the Temple Mount, tourists can plainly see the original limestone foundation blocks cut by King Herod. Ari suddenly turned to Mark as they walked single file down the narrow stone corridor and said, "Whenever I walk on these paver stones, I feel that I have walked on this ancient street before. I almost feel that I'm home." As Ari said this, Mark remembered the image in his mind when he first met and shook hands with Ari. But he said nothing. The tour ended peacefully at the same place it began.

Ari now gave Mark a look signifying that the *real* tour would begin if they could shake Alisa. So Mark casually mentioned to Alisa that he and Ari wanted to do some shopping in the Old City and that he thought she needn't follow. Alisa, reading through Mark's nonchalance, insisted on staying. As Mark and Ari walked quickly through a huge shopping street crowded with tourists and locals, Alisa had trouble keeping up with them. In fact, due to the crowds, she found it hard to see them at times. Alisa's predicament did not come as a surprise to Ari who knew the crowds would be heavy at this time of day.

In a move that surprised Mark, Ari grabbed Mark's arm and quickly yanked him off the busy street. He led him into a narrow alleyway between two ancient stone houses. Because it was so narrow, the two had to walk sideways most of the way. Mark could hear his metal belt buckle scraping against the hard limestone walls and knew that if the alleyway got any narrower, he would be forced to hold his breath and suck in his stomach. Otherwise, he was afraid he might get stuck there! Finally, the narrow space opened up to an ancient stone stairway that was completely worn down with use. The two men quickly disappeared into the darkness down the stairway.

This left a bewildered Alisa all alone and looking everywhere for them. She felt she was more angry with herself for losing sight of those two amateurs than with them. Throughout the day she had a strong feeling that Mark and Ari would try something like this. Luckily, she had slipped a tracking device into Mark's sun cap when he wasn't looking. But she would have to return to her office in Tel Aviv to watch the monitor that could track him! This time, she had stupidly not brought the state of the art tracking device which she could read on her cellphone!

After about fifteen minutes walking, using their flashlights when necessary, Ari led Mark to the tunnel where he had first heard the sound of a trumpet. He turned to Mark when they arrived and said, "This is where I heard the trumpet the loudest. Let's see if we can find what's making the sound and where it's coming from?"

"So it's a bit of a treasure hunt then?" Mark responded.

"Yes, that's why you're here. If anyone can find something, it's you. Besides, I feel a lot better now that you are with me. I was scared to do this alone," Ari confessed. Mark's interest was piqued, especially when he thought he could again hear the sound of a trumpet. He stood listening and surveying the area for a few minutes.

"Do you hear that too?" Mark asked.

"Yes."

"Well, at least I'm not going crazy," Mark replied. As they walked along the tunnel, they both realized the sound was getting louder—it seemed the trumpet was guiding them to its origin by getting louder and clearer the closer they came. "I think the sound is coming from behind this wall. Do you agree?" Mark asked.

Ari replied, "Yes. But there is a problem. This is the outer wall of the Temple Mount, meaning the sound is coming from under the Temple Mount which is an area forbidden to us." This is where Mark's treasure hunting instinct kicked in—no stupid law was going to stop him. "It looks like there was an opening here that was sealed up," Mark said as he shined his flashlight along the wall. "I guess we're at bedrock level, meaning that this opening was cut from the bedrock underneath the outer Temple Mount wall."

"Maybe it was a sewer or drainage channel," Ari said. "It's big enough for us to get through if we're on all fours, one at a time. First let me take a closer look at what's sealing it."

Ari took out his pocket knife, crouched down and began tapping the wall. As soon as he tapped it, the sealant in the wall began to crack and fall away in small chunks. "This part of the wall is blocked with clay, not stone," Ari said. Mark quickly joined him digging into the clay with a pen he found in his pocket. As both men dug, they could hear the beautiful trumpet sound coming from the newly created opening in the wall. About twenty minutes later, they had a big enough hole that someone could fit their head in to see what was on the other side. Mark advised caution, however. "Poisonous air can accumulate in enclosed spaces like this over long periods of time," he said. "We should widen the hole a bit more and wait at least thirty minutes for the bad air to dissipate by mixing with the new air."

They widened the hole, but neither one of them had the patience to wait thirty minutes. They both noticed a slight breeze flowing from the newly cut hole which meant there was an opening somewhere letting in fresh air. So after about fifteen minutes they recklessly broke open the remaining section of the wall and crawled into the newly discovered tunnel with their cellphone flashlights lighting their way. Mark went first. He thought the air smelled musty, but not fowl or harmful. After about ten minutes of crawling along what they thought was a water or sewer channel coming from inside the Temple Mount, they came upon a turn in the tunnel. By then, they were directly under the Temple Mount. As Mark put his hand down on the ground to feel his way ahead, he felt something round and long. He yelled back to Ari that he thought he found something. They both noticed that the moment he touched it the sound of the trumpet stopped. Without waiting to discuss the oddity of the music stopping, Ari yelled to Mark, "Just grab it and let's back up and get out of here!"

But Mark had the same problem with this long thin trumpet or horn that Ari's ancestor had encountered – it was too long to make the turn in the tunnel. Mark thought it was probably about five feet (1.5m) or more in length. With his cellphone flashlight, Mark surveyed the opening and how the tunnel turned to come up with a solution. He took a chance and moved two stones in the tunnel wall just enough at the corner where it turned—praying the ceiling wouldn't collapse on them as he did it. He successfully created enough space for the long object to make the turn but did not want to risk scratching the object. So he slowly backed out of the tunnel on his hands and knees, gently pulling along after him whatever it was he had found. Ari also backed up in lockstep.

Fifteen minutes later Mark and Ari were sitting on the floor of the larger tunnel outside this drainage channel to catch their breath. Both were dirty and tired but also thrilled. Finally they both stood up and Mark Cohn handed this blackened long thing encrusted with more than two millennium of dirt and tarnish to Ari to see if he could discover what it was.

All people with the name of Cohn and other Cohn name derivatives are also descendants of the Jewish hereditary Kohanim or priestly class. By Orthodox Jewish law they are the only ones who are permitted to touch God's Holy Trumpet. What had just occurred – when one descendant of the Jewish priestly class gave the trumpet to another descendant of the Jewish High Priests – had not happened in over two thousand years. As soon as Ari's hands held the trumpet it began to quiver. In fact, like magic the trumpet vibrated, shaking off all the tarnish and dirt that had accumulated on it and strengthening its ancient metal to feel like new. They both looked at what Ari was holding in amazement to see a bright, shiny solid silver trumpet. So bright and shiny that they could see their faces in it!

"It's a miracle!" Mark blurted out.

"Yes, it is. But it's God's miracle," Ari said. "Let me try and play it." With that, he blew on the Holy Trumpet and played it for a little over a minute. "It plays perfectly, like it was new," Ari said. "This must be the Holy Trumpet which is the biblical name for horn, from the Temple described in my family's legend. The legend says that our founder took it from the Temple before it could be looted by the Romans and the Temple burned. I knew it was here when I heard it, but I needed your help—someone who could also hear its sound to find it. Thank you for your help. Now, I think it's time to leave."

But before they moved an inch, Mark held up his hand as if to stop Ari in his tracks. "If this is what we think it is—the true Trumpet from the Holy Temple—you must realize that it is the most important archeological discovery in Jerusalem in over two thousand years," Mark said. "I remember reading that it was used to call millions of Jews to prayer at the Temple Mount. But originally, a thousand years before that, the Bible says it could be blown by the High Priest to call the Hebrew tribes to a God sanctioned war or what we now call Holy War. The Bible also says it could be used by the High Priest to call the Lord God Himself to war in defense of His Chosen people. So, I guess it could also be used as an incredibly powerful weapon by the right person. You also realize we found it under the Temple Mount where we were forbidden to go. And not notifying the authorities that we found it is also against the law. So what are we going to do with it?"

"Mark my friend, take it down a notch," Ari said. "First, God has not manifested Himself in thousands of years. And I sincerely doubt He will do so anytime soon. Second, I will keep the Trumpet safe at my place until we figure this all out." Mark was a little taken aback by the strength in Ari's voice. So, he begrudgingly agreed since he never much cared for Israel's strict archeological laws anyway.

Ari put the Trumpet under his arm and they both walked to the surface and into the sunlight. Walking along the busy streets of Old Jerusalem, Mark turned to his young friend

Ari and said, "I had a fun afternoon. I hadn't been treasure hunting in years."

"I want to thank you again for your help," Ari replied. "I couldn't have found it without you."

As Mark walked away, he shouted to Ari, "Make sure you take a shower when you get home! You look and smell like you just crawled out from a sewer!"

"Look who's talking!" Ari replied with a smile. They both returned to their respective homes with smiles on their faces.

However, they both failed to notice, due to being underground, that when Ari played the trumpet under the Temple Mount, a small, ominous black storm cloud with a bolt of lightning running through it had immediately formed over the Temple Mount on an otherwise clear sunny day. The cloud dissipated just as quickly when Ari stopped playing. While looking back on the day, they were both surprised by how easily they found the long lost trumpet. It almost seemed to them as if the Trumpet itself, or maybe even God, meant for them to find it. But then again, they knew that He sometimes works in strange ways!

As Ari carried the Holy Trumpet through the streets of Jerusalem, they both also failed to notice the trail of people behind them who stopped, turned and bowed their heads towards them while offering a prayer to the Lord. They had not yet realized the power of spirituality the Holy Trumpet unleashed.

Aaron ben Halevi put the Holy Trumpet in his small car, leaning it across the passenger seat all the way back to his apartment in Tel Aviv. In his apartment he leaned it against the corner of his bed's headboard until he could give it some attention. The only thing in his life that had recently changed was his continued intense desire to study the Torah which he did, alone in his apartment every chance he got after practicing with his band or playing at the club. He slept soundly every night close to his new shiny silver trumpet. He was extremely busy studying or playing in his band, so he had not touched the trumpet or given it much thought since he had brought it home.

A week later, everything in his life changed. Because of the next day's very busy schedule, he decided to shower and wash before he went to sleep instead of in the morning. So he slept completely clean. During the night he tossed and turned in bed, causing the trumpet to fall from the corner of his bed's headboard and land on the side of his mattress. While asleep Ari turned so that his hand accidentally covered the mouthpiece end of the trumpet. That night he had a vivid dream that the Lord God spoke to him saying, "You will be Our Hand. We will be with you as We were with your ancestors Moses and

Aaron and Joshua. You will give Our warning to the Prime Minister, the leader of My People that what he is creating is an abomination in Our eyes and he must desist or suffer Our Wrath. Only one time will We give this warning." Ari awoke from his dream in a cold sweat thinking he had gone mad. His eyes widened from his sleep state when he saw that his hand was touching, indeed at this point grasping, the Holy Silver Trumpet. He was very unnerved by his dream but understood he must do what God commanded. However, he didn't know how or where or when to deliver the warning. But he was determined to figure it out! He had first thought his study of the Holy Books was just curiosity. But he now realized he was on his own spiritual search for God. However, in spite of his dream he was still unsure of himself and his faith in God.

CHAPTER NINE

THE WEDDING

Miriam Jansen had been a stunningly beautiful woman when she was younger. And even now, older and the mother of two sons—one a Colonel in the Israeli Defense Forces who was married with three children making her a proud grandmother and the other now Prime Minister married to Mark Cohn—she was still a strikingly beautiful lady. Jacob Kurtz had taken one look at her when they first met on the plane he rented for his son's wedding reception in New York City and had fallen head over heels in love. However, she proved not to be an easy catch. It had taken him more than three years and some serious courting to convince her to marry him. She didn't want to make a mistake again like her first marriage. Her first husband, Eric's father, now lived in Holland. He had turned out to be a blond bastard, leaving her without notice to raise two small children alone. She was definitely not inviting him to her wedding!

She was a no-nonsense type of person who was not impressed with Jacob's wealth or serious political contacts. She had totally accepted her son Eric's marriage to Mark because she felt that Mark was a kind person and would be kind to her son. She knew Eric needed kindness and goodness in his life because of the rough and dangerous career he had chosen within the military to defend Israel. She also knew that Eric was extremely intelligent and could be difficult, if not impossible, to handle at times. Moreover, she knew that Mark was no pushover and was up to the task of making her son happy. So far, her instincts proved correct. But recently she sensed that something was not right with Eric. However, she couldn't put her finger on what it was. She was so busy with her new beau, Jacob, and their wedding that she just didn't have time to focus on it. She simply thought it was the pressures of his new job as Prime Minister.

Even if you hire a wedding planner, which they did, there were still a hundred decisions to be made for the wedding such as venues, guest lists, menus, photographers, decorations, invitations, gowns for the bride and bridesmaids, etc. These decisions were especially crucial for Jacob Kurtz's wedding, where the political elite of Israel and Hollywood would jostle for an invitation due to Jacob's prestigious media company. Also, the fact that the son of the bride was the current Prime

Minister didn't lessen but increased the need for everything to be perfect! Both Jacob and Miriam knew it was going to be a really big affair—the social event of the year for Israel.

With enormous help from their wedding planner and the fact that Miriam was marrying a hugely wealthy man meaning they had a virtually unlimited budget with which to work, the wedding preparations were proceeding nicely. It was going to be a three day affair with six hundred guests invited. Bookings of hotel room blocks were made both at the Mamilla Hotel in Jerusalem and the Norman Hotel in Tel Aviv with limos, vans and buses based on guest preferences ready to shuttle all guests. It is an Israeli tradition to give a cash wedding present. However, the wedding invitation expressly told the quests that no wedding presents were allowed. The names of two Israeli charities were mentioned if anyone wanted to make a contribution in the couples name.

Finally, the wedding weekend arrived. Dinner on the first night was held in the ballroom of the Renaissance Hotel in Jerusalem and included 600 guests. The ballroom walls were covered in white roses and white orchids plus eight foot (2.4m) banquet table displays of flowers as well as sets of baccarat crystal glasses and the finest porcelain dinnerware. There were world famous singers, entertainment and dancing to 2 a.m. There were also a couple of tables for the children that closed down much earlier. The food served was all kosher. The guests included the ambassadors and spouses from the United States, France, Great Britain, India and Morocco as well as the heads of major Hollywood studios. Mark and Eric sat at the bride and grooms table along with Eric's brother David and his wife, and Jacob's son, Ariel and daughter-in-law Julie. Ariel and Julie, now had three children and their marriage looked like a success. Mark was delighted with this and supported their marriage in any way he could, since he knew that Julie dated Eric before he met Mark. To Mark, Julie's successful marriage to a good friend meant no back sliding! Both Eric and Julie knew that their previous relationship still bothered Mark a bit. So they took every opportunity to make sure that he knew they were just friends.

The next day the wedding ceremony was held outside of the city in the barren Judean Hills on the edge of the Negev desert. The wedding planner's company had created a site that looked like something out of an Arabian Nights fantasy combined with a Moroccan palace. Huge white tents with imported palm trees and ferns and an artificial lake with a fountain in the middle made it look like a manicured desert oasis. The theme was white, so everyone wore white. White clothes were provided for every guest if they didn't have a white outfit. Eric's mother walked down the aisle with her son to the Chuppah (a traditional tabernacle under which Jews marry) intertwined with white orchids and white roses, where Jacob Kurtz was waiting along with the rabbi who was going to marry them. The whole crowd was enraptured to see Miriam and Jacob kiss after the rabbi finished the ceremony. And when Jacob stepped on the glass cup to break it (a Jewish custom symbolizing that they would be married for as many years as it takes to put this glass cup back together), the whole crowd applauded. And then the festivities of eating drinking and dancing started under the desert sky filled with stars. As it got dark, all the barren Judean Hills and cliffs surrounding them were lit with thousands of candles creating a joyous wonderland back drop for the party. When Mark had the chance to congratulate Miriam and Jacob on their marriage, he said, "Mazel Tov, Congratulations. And I think your Chanel wedding dress is just fabulous!"

"I am so glad you noticed," Miriam responded happily. "I looked at two dozen dresses but when I saw this Chanel I fell in love with it."

At that point, Eric bent his head toward Mark and said softly, "What's a Chanel?"

Mark gave him a look of utter sympathy saying, "I will tell you later." Hearing this, Miriam just smiled and walked away with her new husband Jacob on her arm. Eric knew from

Mark's look that he was going to get at least an hour long lecture on women's fashion when they got home. A lecture in which he would have to pretend to be interested. But the truth was that he couldn't care less what women wore. He was sorry he asked the question.

During the party, Eric and Mark also met Alexander ben Halevi and his wife, Maya. They stood talking, having a very pleasant conversation, when Mark noticed what Maya was wearing on her finger.

"I wore this ring just for you. I knew I would run into you here," she said as she raised her hand to give Mark a better look.

Mark took a close look and exclaimed, "It's a blue diamond just like the one I found in King Herod's tomb. I am shocked that there is a second stone like it."

"Yes, when I visited the museum Jacob built to house the treasure I was shocked as well," Maya replied. "This sister stone has been in my husband's family for centuries. It looks like Baby Blue, the name you gave the diamond you found, has a sister!"

Mark stared at the stone in amazement. "Do you realize that we are the only two people alive who have actually worn these stones?" Mark asked.

"Yes. Quite a privilege," Maya replied.

"Yes, I believe the two stones come from the same diamond mine in India," Alexander added. "Our founder

Ari ben Halevi got control of that mine two thousand years ago, around the time of King Herod as far as we can tell. There are many legends about our founder. He claimed that God blessed him and that God would even speak to him. My son, who you met, was named after him." Mark instantly connected these legends to his new friend Ari. Mark became very quiet, letting the others in the group carry on the polite party conversation. Mark was beginning to understand who his new young friend actually was. He asked himself, *was Ari some kind of modern day of prophet?*

The entire wedding and three day party was an illusion put together to enhance Eric's political career. Jacob and Miriam had been married in a civil ceremony two days before. But Jacob, Miriam and Eric had thought that a major wedding and religious ceremony would generate excellent publicity for Eric and help bolster his religious credentials amongst the voters. Also, the exotically beautiful location in the desert had not only been chosen for its beauty but for its excellent security in such an isolated desert location. The press was encouraged in to take photos. As expected, the publicity and goodwill generated from his mother's wedding burnished Eric's credentials as the most loved and respected Israeli Prime Minister by the public in decades. He was at the height of his political power with more and more senior military and police positions staffed with people personally loyal to him as well as his secret robot army growing daily. Thus, the wedding was really a methodically staged three day political event to enhance his image.

The last event was a lunch planned at the Mamilla Hotel in Jerusalem. It was a scaled down affair for only 260 people—the ballroom capacity. The guest list included Eric's most important political and religious supporters and their wives in addition to the bride and groom's families. It was where Ari ben Halevi's band was scheduled to play. Previously, their wedding meeting planner had visited Ari's club to hear him and his band play and agreed that they were excellent. Both the meeting planner and Miriam thought a bit of soft jazz would be perfect for the last day's lunch after two nights of eating, drinking and dancing.

After his band finished their last musical set for the wedding lunch, Ari ben Halevi took a deep breath to steady himself and calmly walked over to the table where Eric, Mark and the rest of their family was sitting. Looking directly at Eric Jensen, the Prime Minister of Israel, Ari introduced himself as Aaron ben Halevi. He then proclaimed in a loud voice filled with the spiritual power of God, "I have a message from the Lord God for you. He says that you are not the Hand of God as Moses, Aaron and Joshua were. He is not with you as He was with them. You have created an abomination in His Eyes and will be punished if you do not desist and repent. This is His only warning to you." The entire ballroom went silent. They all heard it. You could hear a pin drop.

Eric realized in this moment that Ari could see his hidden self—his black side. He could see exactly who he really was. Eric felt more enraged than surprised. He thought to himself that a ray gun death would be too quick for his accuser, this man who had just publicly embarrassed him in front of his family and key supporters. For a moment, but just a moment, he seriously thought of crucifying him. But after a minute of feigning surprised silence he regained control of his rage. Now a new feeling of paranoia enveloped him. All these feelings passed through him while being acutely aware of how exposed to the public he was. All he really remembered from what this young man had said was the name Joshua. *How did this man know that he was building a secret robot army of soldiers called Joshua?* He leaped to the conclusion that there must be leak from a traitor.

However, from the outside, looking at him, all his family and friends could see was a stunned look on their Prime Minister's face. Slowly, as his emotional defense mechanism took over, an amused smile formed on Eric's lips as he regained his composure. "Young man, I think you have had too much wine," he calmly said to Ari. "I know your father. So for his sake I will not have you arrested but you must leave here now." With that he raised his hand slightly and his security surrounded Ari and walked him out of the hotel. The rest of his band members were also thrown out. As Ari was leaving, both men's eyes locked. Both men now knew this would be a fight to the death. What the public did not see was that Ari shook nervously from the experience until he arrived home and held the Silver Trumpet. Somehow holding it calmed him and fortified him.

After that incident, everyone at the table started to talk at once. They all thought the man was either drunk or high on some kind of drug. Within a couple of minutes, they were all joking about it—not taking what the young man said seriously. The only person who was not joking around was Mark. He knew enough about Ari ben Halevi to take him dead seriously. Mark silently asked himself the question, *Had God turned against his partner? His partner who he loved more than life itself. How could this be? What was this abomination Ari was talking about?* Mark made up his mind that the first chance he got, he would find his friend Ari and ask him to explain.

Beyond the two tables of family and close friends were guests that consisted of political allies in the Knesset and political parties—many of them religious Jews. These guests had also heard Ari's warning, and did not so easily shake it off.

The spiritual power of Ari's voice and what he said stayed with them long after they left the banquet hall. It forced them to start questioning their support for this Prime Minister. Eric Jansen did not know it then, but this was the beginning of the political fight of his life.

CHAPTER TEN

ABOMINATION

What upset Eric the most was that out of nowhere, this young man was able to easily pierce his outward persona and see his black side. No one before this was able to see the real him unless Eric allowed them to see it. On the ride home in the Prime Minister's limousine, Mark could see that Eric was upset. But he didn't know how to help him. Eric wasn't talking. His paranoia was covering him in waves made worse by his PSTD delusions of traitors all around him. Both Brigadier General Gil Sofer and Colonel Elon Dagen had been keeping him updated but he now thought it was past time for a personal review of his robot army project. He told Mark that he needed to sleep alone that night in his bedroom because he was leaving extremely early the next day. He texted Gil Sofer that he wanted to meet him and Elon Dagen for a major review of the project first thing the next morning. Eric would get to the bottom of who was leaking information! The robot and aerial battleship projects were no longer located at the Technion Institute in Haifa or scattered at different locations around the country but had been consolidated at a secret robot production center in the Negev. So the meeting was set for there. Gill Sofer texted the directions of this secret facility to Eric Jansen. Eric memorized the location then deleted the text.

The isolated robot production facility in the middle of Negev desert had been built with funds provided by Alexander ben Halevi, Ari's father. The irony of that was completely lost on Eric in his current mental state. He drove there alone without any security guards so as to keep the location secret. While driving he tried desperately to control his paranoia and anger brought on by the thought that someone had leaked his robot project and betrayed him. When he arrived at the entrance of this secret production facility, he admired how the entrance was designed not to draw attention to itself. In fact, the entrance was an old metal door to what looked like a dusty old bunker. Its exterior also looked like it had been allowed to fall into disrepair, half hidden with desert sand. The old metal door squeaked when he pushed it open but automatically closed behind him. There were five rusty steps leading down to another door. This door was also metal but shined like aluminum. As he stood in front of it in the darkness, a beam of red light above the door scanned his face and body measurements. It only took three seconds to confirm who he was. Then the metal door slid open revealing a sleek modern elevator. The elevator door almost instantly closed behind him, quickly descending four floors.

When the elevator door opened he was greeted by an almost seven foot (2.1m) tall robot that immediately said, "Greetings, Creator. Please follow me." It led him through a hallway to a conference room door which it opened. Sitting at the end of the conference table was Brigadier General Gil Sofer who stood immediately when he saw the Prime Minister enter. The General was first to speak saying, "Good morning. Welcome to our production facility. We were lucky to find this big underground ancient cave system carved from rushing water. It expedited the facility's construction. Would you like some coffee?"

"No thank you," Eric said, cutting him off. "I want to start my review as soon as possible."

"Of course," the General responded. "Colonel Dagen will be here very shortly. But while I have you alone, I need to update you about certain things happening here. Please sit." They both sat in chairs close to one another as the General continued. "To begin with, there are no cameras, listening or recording devices in this room so we can speak freely. I want you to know our production of these robots is ahead of schedule. We now have completed more than 1200 hundred robot soldiers plus four robots which we call leaders. We now have a full production line of robots making robots. The number of robot soldiers double every week. We also have successfully miniaturized our battleship laser weapon into a handheld weapon. We also have robots constructing five more aerial battleships. But this is what I want to warn you about. The newer robots are smarter and stronger than the original robots. So much so they have created leaders among themselves without our approval. The newer ones have made improvements on the older ones so that now they all learn by touching one another. Remember that Colonel Dagen told you their memory and intelligence is a series of electrical impulses. So now, when one robot touches another these impulses are transmitted within seconds. For example, we taught our original robot, Joshua, all our most advanced personal defense military combat techniques. All he did was touch the arm of the next robot and all the information was transferred and so on and so on. So when one of them learns something new, they all know it within minutes simply by touching one another. And lastly, I think the four new leader robots are actually sentient or soon will be, meaning they think for themselves without our direction. In my opinion they cannot be controlled. I have taught them all I know. They now can assemble and pilot aerial Dragon Fire battleships faster and better than any human. And they have made improvements to the laser weapons that have astounded even me. For instance, the robots have improved the range of fire by our battleship lasers to fifty miles (80.5km) above the earth with an accurate destructive target width of over three miles (4.8km). I also think that the leader robots are showing signs of communication by mental telepathy, not needing to touch the others to transmit directions anymore. I think they are trying to hide that mental ability from us. Therefore, I think they have become too dangerous, and the program should be discontinued until we have time to study them further."

While sitting there listening intently to General Gil Sofer, Eric Jansen came to three conclusions from what he heard. First, he was extremely pleased that such progress had been made with his robot army and aerial battleships. Eric thought the Joshuas were now ready for combat. However, over his own dead body would he stop this program at this stage. Secondly, he was completely convinced that the General was the person who leaked the information about the robots. And thirdly, since the General had taught the Joshuas all he knew, Eric didn't really need him anymore.

Eric now stood up and said in his most sincere voice to General Sofer, "You have covered a great many things. I will need time to think about what you have just told me. But now I need a tour of the place." He turned towards the door but stopped so the General could lead the way. The General stood up, considerably more relaxed thinking the meeting had gone well and that the Prime Minister would seriously consider discontinuing the program. General Sofer had taken two steps past Eric when Eric grabbed him from behind and put his big right hand over Gil Sofer's mouth while simultaneously pinching his nostrils closed with two fingers. His left hand grabbed his neck and shoulders, forcing him back. The surprise attack by the Prime Minister took the General completely off guard. Eric Jansen was still a master assassin trained by the Mossad. Four minutes later General Gil Sofer was dead from suffocation, laying sprawled across the conference table. This Mossad killing technique left no scars on the body and looked like the victim had died of a heart attack. But what made Eric Jansen a master assassin was when he bent over the body and arranged Gil Sofer's hands to look like he was clutching his chest above his heart to give everyone the strong impression of a heart attack. As Eric looked at the dead body on the table before him, he felt his paranoia drain from him. He also felt satisfied. He had not killed in a long while and there was a part of him that always enjoyed it.

He waited another minute to compose himself then ran to the door for help, yelling, "I think General Sofer had a heart attack. He needs help!" Several soldiers appeared from nowhere and rushed into the room. One tried to resuscitate him.

Colonel Elon Dagen rushed into the room soon after with an utterly surprised look on his face. When he saw the medical officer on duty arrive and pronounce the General dead, he realized what was happening was beyond his control. "I am so sorry this happened to Gil," the Colonel said to Eric. "But no one told me you were coming today or I would have been here to greet you." Eric was watching Elon's every move and listening to every nuance in his voice. He asked himself, *Did Gil Sofer inform him, or not?* It really didn't matter anymore. His assessment was that he had eliminated the right one.

"I want Brigadier General Sofer to be buried with full military honors," Eric told Elon. "His work was invaluable in the defense of the country. I will plan to attend the funeral. And General Dagen, I still need to have a tour of this place, today."

Elon Dagen looked straight at the Prime Minister and with much respect said, "Sir, I am a Colonel, not a General."

"Not anymore, you are now the Brigadier General in charge of the whole program. I will inform the military High Command tomorrow of my decision to promote you."

"Thank you, Mr. Prime Minister," Elon said. "I'm your man. I won't fail you."

"Good. Now show me my army!"

Soon to be the new Brigadier General, Elon Dagen led his Prime Minister along another corridor through a set of double doors. As they entered a huge three story underground chamber Elon told Eric, "I have taught them a new greeting for their Creator. I hope you like it."

Eric walked out to a small platform looking over the rest of the room with Elon two steps behind him. Below the platform were more than 1200 seven foot (2.1m) tall Joshua robots with the four leader robots standing there as well. As soon as Eric entered the room, the robots raised their stiff right arms in the old style fascist salute and shouted six times in unison, "Hail Creator!" Eric couldn't help himself when this show of absolute loyalty and respect brought a small tight smile to his lips. Standing there above his robot soldiers, he allowed himself a moment to bathe in the rush of power flowing over him of a killer robot army personally loyal to him. As he slowly raised his right arm to return their salute, a tiny, a really very tiny, small thought popped into his mind and refused to go away. As a well trained archeologist, this salute he was returning to his robot soldiers reminded him not of fascists but of the salute the Roman legions gave to Caesar, their Emperor. In his mind, he asked himself, *Why not recreate the Roman Empire by conquering every country on the Mediterranean Sea—to close the circle again. But this time with Jerusalem not Rome, as the capital! With robot legions like this, who could stop me?* This new thought scared him. It was so audacious. A thought he would never say out loud. Nevertheless, the thought would not go away and it made him feel giddy with excitement. It became his secret thought for now! He had never felt better. In fact, he felt elated as if he was floating with his destiny unfolding before him. Whether he knew it or not, he was starting to experience an example of the old expression, "Power corrupts, and absolute power corrupts absolutely."

After a few minutes of surveying the scene from the platform, he turned to Elon Dagen and the four leader robots, saying, "I need to have a discussion with you about our next steps. Where would be a good place?" Elon Dagen promptly said the conference room where they just came from would be ideal. They all returned to the conference room. Elon Dagen was relieved to see the medical officer had already removed Gil Sofer's body.

When Eric and Elon were both seated at the conference table and the four robots, each called Leader, were standing by the two creators, Eric was the first person to begin the discussion.

"I do not like the name Leader," he said as he pointed at the robots. "In the future you will be known as Captain 1, Captain 2, Captain 3, and Captain 4. As we grow you can add on numbers to the title of Captain. Also all robot soldiers must be given a number so they can be immediately identified."

The four robots replied in unison, "By your command, Creator."

Eric continued, "I have heard that you have not been tested in real combat yet. Is that true?"

"Yes, Creator," they replied.

"Therefore, you must be tested," Eric began. "I have picked a site. It is a geographical location in the country of Yemen. About 70% the country is controlled by a group of people called the Houthis who are Israel's sworn enemies. Half of the territory they control is remote mountains with caves and desert that are very removed from modern communication devices. But do not underestimate them. The people there are trained in guerrilla warfare and heavily armed with fortified bunkers and fortified weapons storage facilities. I believe there are approximately 9 million people in the back-country area that I am talking about. No one knows for sure because no one has ever done an exact census. This specific target territory does not include the coastal areas and cities where there are far more communication devices and thus the possibility of discovery. Your prime direction for this combat battle test is for it to be kept secret. I am not ready for the world to know about you yet. My other directive is for you to incinerate the entire population. No Prisoners. I want you to develop a battle plan for this and implement it. You may take as many soldiers and material with you as you need." Eric then turned to Elon and asked, "Do you have any problems with my directions for this test? Or anything to add?"

"No problems," Elon replied.

The Captain 1 robot now asked permission to speak to the Creator, which was given. He then said, "In two days time we will have five fully functional Dragon Fire aerial battleships with full laser weapon capability. However, we can also use them as troop carriers as well as battleships until we can build airborne troop carriers. After landing our troops we can use the battleships for reconnaissance and targeting instead of drones. They will hover 20 miles (32.1km) above the earth, hidden from human detection. According to our tests they have better acuity of vision than any existing drone technology even at that height. Creator, do we have your permission to proceed?"

"Yes, you have my permission to proceed," Eric replied. The robot captains stood there for a minute, analyzing the commands they had just been given.

Then Captain 1 asked another question, "What is the time frame for the completion of this battle test?"

"As soon as you are ready it should be completed. Meaning as soon as possible," Eric responded.

"By your command," Captain 1 said.

Eric Jansen stood up, signaling that the meeting was over. On the way out he said to Elon Dagen, "Keep me posted on every detail. If this goes wrong we are both screwed. I will review your actual robot production areas next time I visit. Congratulations General, so far you have done a brilliant job." Both Eric and Elon failed to notice that only one Joshua robot was asking the questions and responding. Already the robots, step by step, were creating their own general—their own leader!

Eric Jansen did not have long to wait. A week later he received a call from Brigadier General Elon Dagen. Eric expected to get a full update on the preparations for the upcoming battle test. Instead Elon said, "Mission completed. We have aerial battleship photos and videos as well as those taken by the Joshuas robots on the ground that verify it was a total success. Your commands were all successfully completed. I do not want to say more over a cellphone. We should meet soon to review."

Eric replied, "I will meet you early—first thing tomorrow where we met last time." They then both hung up.

Eric was ecstatic. He thought to himself that now is the time to implement the next stage of his plans, but not before a thorough review with Elon tomorrow. He also thought it was time to reconnect with Mark who he had been neglecting because he had been legitimately very busy governing the country. He knew what would make a good impression on Mark. He entered their home that night holding a big bouquet of flowers which he gave to Mark without saying a word. Mark took one look at those flowers and a smile lit up his face, knowing it was going to be a night of love making. Eric smiled inwardly, thinking that he could manipulate Mark or the Israeli Knesset (parliament) as easy as spinning a dreidel—a child's four sided toy top. However, without wanting to or being aware of it, Eric had also developed an emotional co-dependency on Mark. He had come to depend on Mark for unflinching love and loyalty in the unstable new political world that surrounded them both. Without Eric knowing it, Mark had become Eric's one weakness.

Mark couldn't bring himself to confess to Eric that he had recently met with his friend Ari and explain what he had learned. He didn't think it was the right moment. But Eric was no fool. He knew Mark so well that he could tell something was on his partner's mind. So with as much gentleness as his voice could muster, Eric asked, "I can tell something is on your mind. Want to talk about it?"

Mark responded without holding back. "After Ari's warning to you at the wedding dinner, I met with him two days later. I still don't know what Ari was referring to when he called what you are doing an abomination. And quite frankly neither does he. I asked him point blank when I met with him what he meant. However-"

Eric cut him off, saying, "I know you're friends with this guy, Aaron ben Halevi, and it's good that you have a young friend. I know that you both played hide and seek in Jerusalem with Alisa who was there for your protection and who was very concerned when you both disappeared. She gave me a full report so I know that when you returned home later in the day covered in dirt and God knows what else that you were climbing around in some underground passage under Jerusalem. I know that by the grin on your face when you got back that you probably found something, especially with your good luck. Maybe you found it under the Temple Mount itself even though it's forbidden to explore there. I know all this because I used to love to go exploring and do the same thing and understand your motivation. But please, if you found something like a coin or something with some writing on it under the city and your friend still has it, ask him to give it to the Director of the Israeli Museum and I will see no criminal charges are filed." At this point Eric stopped to see if Mark was following him. Eric very gently placed his forefinger under

Mark's chin to close Mark's mouth that had dropped open a bit along with the stunned look on his face.

Mark didn't say a thing in response, which Eric took to mean that Mark understood what he had just been told. So Eric continued, "As for your friend Ari and his outburst at the wedding dinner, have you ever heard of the Jerusalem Syndrome?" Mark shook his head from side to side indicating that he had not. Eric continued again saying, "It affects some people when they visit Jerusalem—about 100 people a year according to our medical records. It affects Christians, Jews and Moslems. It is mental psychosis that results when you become intoxicated with the city. Sometimes people believe they have become biblical figures such as Jesus or Moses or the Temple High Priest. It is a delusional state that clears up after they leave the city or Holy land. In my opinion your friend Ari clearly suffers from this. So please don't take him seriously." Eric could plainly see that Mark was stunned by what he just told him.

So, to switch gears and lighten the mood between them, Eric hugged Mark tightly saying, "Did I ever tell you that you are the love of my life?" As Eric knew it would, this snapped Mark out of his stunned state of mind and back into the here and now and into Eric's arms. What followed was indeed a night of love making. However, Eric never told Mark that

Alisa had put a tracking device on him. Eric figured that there was no sense stirring those waters!

Early the next morning Eric Jansen drove himself to the secret production site of his robot army in the Negev desert. As Mark was left alone in bed after Eric departed, he began to process what Eric had told him the night before about his friend Ari. For a while he thought he was foolish to worry about Eric and the warning Ari had issued at the wedding. That was until the thought occurred to him that he had never verbally mentioned the office of the High Priest of the Temple to Eric. Therefore, for Eric to put it on the same level as Jesus and Moses was very odd. The only way Eric would have chosen that as an example was if he had seen the image of Ari as High Priest when he shook Ari's hand in the club. All the soothing that Eric had done last night to put Mark at ease became undone with this thought. Mark knew something was not right and he went on full alert.

Eric Jansen entered the well hidden secret entrance of his robot production facility and was led by the newest version of the Joshua robot to Brigadier General Elon Dagen and the Captain 1 Joshua robot who were waiting for him in the conference room. This time only the Captain 1 robot was there representing the army. Eric immediately took a seat and commanded Captain 1 robot to report. It said, "Our Yemeni battlefield test operation was a success. By our count 8,927,413 humans were incinerated and no one in the country knows how it happened or who or what did it. We accomplished it in total secrecy. We attribute this to the total surprise of our attack with our advanced weapons and training. Our handheld laser guns performed very proficiently as expected. Our aerial battleships were placed at altitudes above the vision of the human eye. In addition to their laser capable weapons, they performed reconnaissance and targeting functions better than the most advanced drone systems. Our Joshua robot soldiers had the opportunity to hone their fighting skills. There were no loses on our side. Here is the file created to show you the details of the hour by hour and minute by minute test battle. Without a doubt, this battle has proven that each Joshua robot is worth at least twenty human soldiers on the battlefield." Both Elon Dagen and Eric Jansen looked at each and smiled.

"Almost nine million of our enemies annihilated in a week with no casualties on our side," Eric said. "Good! I'm impressed. Now let's see what happens next with Yemen."

Eric then said to robot Captain 1, "Do you have any recommendations for improvement or military equipment needed for future battles?"

"Creator, since our last communication a week ago our soldier robot number more than doubled to 2500 units ready for combat," Captain 1 replied. "We are running up against raw mineral scarcity to maintain our production levels. Therefore, by your command, I wish to use one of our aerial battleships to explore the nearby circling body which is called the moon for mineral deposits needed for production. We have the trained soldier robots capable of piloting such a mission. This will avoid any complications with existing power centers on earth that currently control the minerals we need. At the same time, I recommend that we draw up plans for three satellites fully armed with our latest laser weapons which can cover every inch of the planet earth. Our upgraded lasers can now effectively hit any earth target at those distances. We simply need the satellite platforms which we can manufacture ourselves."

Eric now turned to Elon and asked him, "How do I know this Captain 1 robot is correct in his analysis?"

Elon then said to Captain 1 robot, "By my command tell us why you are correct in your analysis."

The robot replied, "Creators, I am an upgraded version of the first Joshua. I am able to strategize and respond with military solutions. I have read and absorbed every book and treatise in their original language on warfare in every military library and military college on the planet. I am unquestionably the foremost military mind and strategist on the planet."

All Eric said was, "Impressive. I will consider your request. Now show me your production areas so I might get a better understanding of your capabilities." With that they started the tour. They first came to the areas where the bodies of the robots were assembled. There were a dozen robots assembling more robots lying on tables. Elon said that originally he used steel to make Joshua 1. But he now uses a composite metal that is stronger and lighter than steel and is better at conducting electricity to send messages throughout the robot body.

After that they arrived at the area where the robot brains were made, or more accurately where the liquid inside the brain cavity was made, before it was injected into the robot brain cavity. They all had to stand outside looking through a glass window into a sterile laboratory room where sterile robots made it. Elon said it was a secret formula that gave the robots memory he alone had developed. All Eric noticed was that it was the color of emerald green with the consistency of Jello. Advanced biophysics applied to robotics was not his strong point.

As they were ending the tour they passed a door with the sign on it that said "Dr. Frankenstein." Elon saw Eric raise an eyebrow when he saw it. Before he could ask the question,

Elon said, "Yes this is my office with all my records and files concerning robot development. Gil Sofer, may he rest in peace, thought it was funny to put that sign up. He had such an odd sense of humor. It was his nickname for me. I have been so busy that I have not had time to take it down. My office also has Gil Sofer's records and files for his development of the antigravity fusion engine for Dragon Fire and all the laser weapon schematics. The room, itself, has double thick reinforced concrete walls making it the safest spot here."

Upon hearing this, Eric burst into laughter regarding Elon's nickname. He immediately apologized, saying to Elon Dagen, "I'm sorry I laughed, but certain things strike me as funny. Mark always told me I have such an odd sense of humor." No matter how Elon tried to hide it, he was not amused. Eric realized walking back to the conference room that no matter what happened between them in the future, his name for Elon Dagen would always be Dr. Frankenstein. Their path back to the conference room lay through the room where all the Joshua robot soldiers stood. As the two Creators walked through, every robot eye followed them. What Eric Jansen couldn't know was that the real reason Gil Sofer had named Elon Dagen Dr. Frankenstein was that he thought Elon Dagen to be a morally bankrupt monster making monster robots with no moral restraints like himself.

When they arrived back at the conference room, they both sat around the conference table with robot Captain 1 standing there ready to serve. Eric started the conversation by saying, "I am impressed with what I saw. I believe we are ready to start stage 2 of my plan. It should occur in approximately three weeks. How many Joshua units can you have armed and ready by then?"

Robot Captain 1 replied, "At least six thousand soldiers equipped with laser guns."

"Delay the moon mineral exploration project until after stage 2 is complete," Eric said. "I believe we will need all Dragon Fire battleships for stage 2. So build as many as you can before we start stage 2."

Robot Captain 1 replied, "By your command, Creator."

Before he left, Eric turned to Brigadier General Elon Dagen and said, "Keep up the good work. We'll talk soon." He knew this compliment was deserved and it would also make Elon feel good. However, he chuckled to himself when he said it, thinking about Elon's nickname. Later from his office, Eric called his friend and the Chief of Mossad operations, Sam Riechman. He told him to tell his contacts in Saudi Arabia to tell their allies in Yemen's central government that now would be the most opportune time to attack the Houthis.

Three days later Eric Jansen met with the Israel Defense Force General Staff and his cabinet to review what was happening in Yemen. The Houthis, an anti-Israel terrorist group, had been overrun and defeated by central government forces who announced the Red Sea would be immediately open to all shipping and all hostilities with Israel would cease. Everyone at the table was dumbfounded at how quick this policy reversal happened. Eric Jansen welcomed the government of Yemen's decision and pretended to be surprised.

CHAPTER ELEVEN

FRIENDS AND ENEMIES

Mark visited Ari at his apartment the day after Mark's odd conversation with Eric. Alisa came along with Mark for his security. Everything was good again between Alisa and Mark since he had apologized to her for giving her the slip the other day. As he and Alisa parked and started walking towards Ari's apartment, he noticed something odd. A large crowd of Orthodox Jews had gathered outside the entrance to Ari's apartment. Many of them were looking up at Ari's window, and the rest were standing still and staring at the building. Mark was able to get through the crowd, but they stopped Alisa and barred her from getting through. Mark yelled back to her, "Wait for me outside. I won't be long."

When his friend Ari opened his apartment door, the first thing Mark said was not hello, but, "Do you see the crowd of Orthodox Jews gathered outside looking up at your window?"

"Yes, I certainly do," Ari responded. "It's a little creepy. Apparently someone took a video of me giving my warning to your husband and the video went viral. When I look at the video I can hardly believe it's me. I really don't like public speaking. I don't think I'm good at it. And just between you and me, I am not sure I believe in God either."

Mark, trying to ignore Ari's confession about his inner struggles, said, "And you sounded different, too. Remember, I was there. It wasn't your normal voice."

"I'm having coffee," Ari said. "Do you want some?" Mark nodded yes. They both sat at his small table drinking coffee and looking out his window at the crowd looking back at them from the street below. Mark was not surprised when Ari told him about his insecurities. Mark had sensed it in Ari when they first met. Ari, changing the subject, continued about the crowd outside saying, "It's worse at the club. They follow me everywhere. They stand outside the club and listen to me play my trumpet. It wouldn't be so bad if they came into the club and spent some money. But they don't. They just stand outside."

"Well, look at the bright side," Mark said. "All these guys surrounding you all the time is good for your security. No one is going to bother you."

"I never thought of it like that. But I still have no privacy with them around."

"Totally understand. I have no privacy too since Eric became political," Mark replied.

They took a few more sips of coffee before Mark began to explain the reason for his visit. "I spoke to Eric about this abomination thing of which you accused him. He said he doesn't know what you're talking about and that you were delusional. He also said he would see that we are not prosecuted if we turned in whatever we found under Jerusalem. He has no idea what we found but he did know we went exploring under the city. For the record, I do not recommend we turn in that silver trumpet. Remember, I heard its music too. I still wonder why the trumpet seemed to lead us to it."

Ari sat motionless thinking of how to respond to his friend. He knew what he was about to say was going to be tough for Mark to hear and could affect their friendship. "Do you think I'm delusional even though I swear to you that I had a dream that the Lord God spoke to me," Ari began. "And I have never told this to anyone but when I awoke from that dream I was accidentally touching the silver trumpet that lay by the side of my bed."

"No, I don't think you're delusional," Mark reassured him. "Both of us are very sensitive to our metaphysical surroundings. That's all."

Ari took a deep breath. "I also have no idea what the abomination is. But when I first met your husband at the club and shook his hand I saw a blackness in him surrounded by evil.

It was so strong it made me shudder. I didn't want to tell you this because I know you truly love him, but he is dangerous. Be careful. And whether he knows it or not he is involved with something that God considers an abomination. If he knows what it is, then he is lying to you." Mark was shocked that his friend Ari, who he considered as metaphysically perceptive as himself, had seen Eric's black side. He thought Eric had buried or minimized that killer part of him that made him such a good Special Forces soldier and Mossad agent years ago. He seriously thought that side of Eric was no longer a factor in their lives. To hear this from Ari made Mark feel woozy. He felt woozy because he connected it to Eric's recent comment about the High Priest. He knew instinctively that what Ari just told him was the truth. The truth being that Eric's killer side was alive and well and directing his actions. He also felt so stupid for not realizing this before and not trying to help Eric fight his black side as they had successfully done together in the past.

Ari saw the pain in Mark's face as he processed what Ari had told him. He felt sad for his friend and took no pleasure from being right about Eric. After a couple of minutes of silence, Mark said, "I need to leave now. Make sure you keep the trumpet safe. We'll speak soon. Thanks for the coffee." When Alisa saw him downstairs she could tell immediately that something was not right with Mark. All he told her was that he thought he may be coming down with the flu and wanted to go home and rest. Driving back home with Alisa, all Mark could think about was what kind of abomination Ari was talking about and how it would affect Eric. He wouldn't rest until he got answers.

To quote Sun Tzu in his book *The Art of War*, "All warfare is based on deception. The best way to achieve victory is to deceive the enemy." And Eric Jansen, Prime Minister of Israel, was a master at deceiving his perceived enemies. The next day, after the political reversal by Yemen's government, Eric Jansen went to see Sam Reichman in his office at Mossad HQ. He knew that Sam, the chief of Israel's vast spy network, would have the private cellphone number of the new President of Syria and a burner phone. He needed both because he didn't trust the Syrians with his own personal cellphone number and wanted to talk directly with him to avoid any misinterpretations or security leaks. After getting both items he departed Mossad Headquarters and called Elon Dagen to tell him that they needed to meet later that same day.

Later that afternoon Eric found himself sitting in the conference room of the secret robot production facility with

Elon and Captain 1 robot to review the next stage of Eric's plans. Eric started by saying, "I want to state the strategic objective of what is going to happen next. I want Israel to invade and conquer the Gaza strip, the country of Jordan, and all of southern Syria up to the outskirts of Damascus. At the same time our robots will invade southern Lebanon and take that as well. I want to use our aerial battleship laser weapons for the first assaults, followed by our Joshua robot units with their laser guns. This is the stage where it will be necessary to reveal the existence of our Joshua robots and our Dragon Fire battleships to the world. However, the exact numbers of our robot forces will still remain top secret. I am also ready for some negative international backlash on Israel from this endeavor."

General Dagen showed a small tight smile on his lips when Eric told him this. He was more than ready for this. Before Eric continued, the General added, "I have made one small modification to our warrior robots that will make them more efficient. Their laser guns are now part of their lower left arm. All they have to do is point their arm and bend their hand back at the wrist to fire. Everything now is connected to the electrical impulse of their brain for a much more efficient operation and all robots have been retrofitted with this." Eric told Elon that he thought it was a brilliant improvement and that Elon was a genius. This compliment made the General almost burst with pride which was very unusual for this very unemotional and calculated man.

Eric then continued, "First we need to start a war between the new government in Syria and the Hashemite monarchy that rules Jordan. It shouldn't be too difficult since they hate each other. The new government in Syria is a group of Islamic terrorists with roots in Al-Qaeda and strong connections to other radical Islamic terrorist groups in our area. They consider the Hashemite monarchy ruling Jordan as too Western and a disgrace to Islam. They also think the same about the two million plus Palestinian refugees living in Jordan. Conversely the Hashemite monarchy thinks the new rulers of Syria are a bunch of barbarian Islamic radicals out to murder them. So up to this point I wanted peace on our borders. But now, I want to start a war. I have given this idea some thought. Captain 1, are you aware of the small dam along the Yarmuk River that feeds the Jordan River and acts as the border between Syria and Jordan?"

"I am aware of the dam and the entire geography of the border area," Captain 1 replied.

"Good. I want you to drop two Joshua robots close to the dam on the Jordanian side of the river," Eric explained. "The dam is an important source of fresh water for the area so it is guarded by Syrian and Jordanian troops each on their respective side of the border. The mission of these two Joshua robots will be to shoot and kill as many Syrian soldiers as possible from the Jordanian side, but not all of them. There must be some remaining alive to tell the story. The two Joshuas are not to be seen by soldiers from either side. You will supply them with the same high powered, long distance military rifles used by the Jordanian army. No laser ray guns are to be used. I need dead soldier bodies this time to be shown on Syrian and world TV. Afterwards the robots must hide themselves until we arrive. No one must see them until then. Hopefully this will be the spark that starts a war. In the meantime, I will get the ball rolling with the Syrians. Any questions or problems that you foresee?"

The Captain 1 robot asked, "What is your time frame for this mission?"

Eric looked directly at the command robot and said, "As soon as you are ready you may proceed."

"By your command, both Joshua units will be dropped tonight and will accomplish their mission the next day," the Captain 1 responded.

Eric replied, "Good. Now, for the next stage of this war between Syria and Jordan we need all available Joshua robots and Dragon Fire battleships to be ready to deploy along our Jordanian border as well as Gaza, Syrian and our northern Galilee border with Hezbollah. I will make sure that everything blows up at once. On my command you will position our troops and aerial battleships at key points along those four borders. We will finish these incessant border wars once and for all with one final war with no Israeli casualties! I will use regular IDF troops to help hold and govern our new territories once our robot troops have swept through and exterminated the enemy population. Remember, no prisoners. Our lasers will incinerate all our enemies so there won't be any dead bodies remaining. I will give you the command when to invade. For the sake of world public opinion, I must be seen to respond to attacks, not start them. Also, I will send you a map today indicating allied villages in southern Syria and Lebanon which must not be touched. I need go now, but when I leave, Brigadier General Dagen is in charge to coordinate this in my absence."

"Creator, with your permission, I recommend that one Dragon Fire battleship be placed in orbit above the planet to shoot down any missiles launched from either Yemen or Iran," Captain 1 suggested.

"Agreed," Eric replied. "If they launch against us, then destroy that country as well."

The command robot replied, "By your command, Creator."

Brigadier General Elon Dagen stood to salute Eric. "We will be ready to go when you say go!" he said. Eric returned his salute and left for his office. He had a lot of work to do to make sure Israel's enemies attacked first so he could be seen as defending his country and not starting a war. Eric Jansen was almost ready to unleash an army of killer robots and aerial battleships with lethal laser weapons the world had never seen!

Eric didn't trust the new leader of Syria. President Abdul-Al-Rahman of Syria had a background steeped in Islamic fanaticism. He had ordered the deaths of thousands of fellow Syrians who didn't agree with his specific radical brand of Islam. However, Abdul-Al-Rahman was not really surprised to get a call from his new neighbor. He immediately recognized the voice on his cellphone as the famous Prime Minister of Israel. Al-Rahman had been reaching out to world leaders trying to legitimize his murderous regime. So he asked himself before he spoke, *Why not speak to the Jew animal leader of a nation of subhumans? A nation, that my Holy Book, the Koran, instructs me to kill or convert. I might learn something useful or detect a weakness.* Eric too, would have been just as glad to put a knife through the Syrian President's heart. It would have made his day to feel his enemy's warm blood gushing over his hand. Both men were acutely aware of how the other felt.

Eric spoke first, introducing himself in fluent Arabic in the friendliest tone he could muster. "Thank you for listening, Mr. President. I am Eric Jansen, the Prime Minister of Israel. I know you are busy so I will be brief. I know you detest the Hashemite monarchy that rules Jordan as much as I do. I believe it is time for a change. If you ever contemplate crossing the Yarmuk River to consolidate your two countries I would not intervene. Israel would remain neutral in such a war. Of course, I think in the future, diplomatic recognition of my country by yours for our neutrality during such a war would be appreciated."

At this point Eric stopped and let the message sink in. Abdul-Al-Rahman was surprised. He had always wanted to expand his power base in the Arab world. But he knew he must proceed very cautiously with his answer. He responded by saying, "Yes, I recognize your voice from your many press conferences as Prime Minister and even before that as a famous archeologist. I believe in a good neighbor policy including Jordan and yourself. But I have a question. The Jordanian King now controls the Waqf (Islamic organization) that administers the Haram al-Sharif (The Temple Mount) in Jerusalem. If the monarchy fell, who would control it?"

Eric knew he had him where he wanted him. So Eric responded, "That, of course, is an internal Arab issue. But as the ruler of the surrounding area of Jerusalem I would always prefer someone with whom I work well."

Abdul-Al-Rahman immediately said, "I need to go now, but I think we should leave this line of communication open."

"Agreed. It has been my honor to speak to you. Good luck," Eric responded. When Eric finished the call, he thought to himself, *Message delivered and understood! Now I just need to wait for the two Joshua snipers to stir the pot.*

Early the next day Eric called for a meeting with the Israel Defense Force High Command for midday that same day. The Chief of the IDF High Command was General Uri Barak. Eric had a great deal of respect for the man. The extremely smart and tough as nails General was a veteran of many wars. Eric knew he had to be on his toes around him. So, to begin the meeting Eric told a couple of off-color military jokes much beloved by soldiers to relax everyone. He then went around the table and asked all the military generals and admirals to report, leaving General Barak for the last. When he got to General Barak, all the general said was, "Get to the point Mr. Prime Minister!"

Eric realized long before this meeting he would lose if he ever played a game of chess with this guy. So Eric replied, "I was thinking it is time for some military war games—training exercises. That's all. Let's pretend that we are invaded from all sides and the goal of the games is to protect Israel by blunting the attacks. But this time with a twist. I want you to respond with an invasion plan for the Gaza strip, the entire country of Jordan and most of southern Syria and southern Lebanon simultaneously. And I want the plan for that on my desk in

48 hours. In the meantime, I know there is no exact number of troops for a military training exercise. So I want you to call up 25,000 veteran reservists for training. Again, I want them called up within twenty-four hours for two weeks of training exercise. There should be no press releases except to say that Israel is holding a small scheduled military training exercise. Gentlemen, make this happen." Eric Jansen then stood up and said he had a cabinet meeting to attend. The whole table stood up and saluted him. He returned their salute and left.

After the Prime Minister departed, all the officers around the table began to discuss what just happened amongst themselves. They were brought to order by General Barak who simply said, "We were just given an order. We must carry it out. However, just to be on the safe side, cancel all leaves for the armed forces for two weeks. And put the officer corp on alert. Do not alert the regular army yet. My gut tells me that there is more to this than we were just told. Or in other words, we must lock and load and be ready without appearing to be ready. Dismissed."

Halfway through Eric's regular scheduled cabinet meeting later that day, the world press announced a major skirmish that was growing into a battle between Jordan and the new government in Syria over water rights to the only dam on the Yarmuk River. Eric Jansen immediately announced in a hastily called press conference his country's neutrality regarding the emerging battle between the two countries. After the press conference Eric called General Dagen and said, "Get ready to deploy soon. Very soon!" then hung up. Eric Jansen also called Mark, leaving a message on his cellphone that he would not be sleeping home that night but would stay at his office, and possibly would have to remain there for several more nights until a minor crisis had passed. He reassured Mark that everything was fine and that he would see him soon. Eric was also very well aware that by publicly announcing he would be sleeping at his office, he was sending a not so subtle message to the entire security establishment of the country to be on unofficial alert.

Mark got Eric's voice message. He took a deep breath to steady himself, knowing everything was not fine with his partner regardless of this message. But for the moment his hands were tied.

The skirmish between the government of Syria and the government of Jordan grew into a major battle with both sides committing more and more troops. The world press started to cover it. Finally, both sides committed their entire country's armed forces. Within three days the Jordanian side started losing the battle to Syria's army soldiers – all of them battle hardened, fanatical, and former ISIS. By the fourth day the

Syrian army started to sweep south and overrun the country, killing almost everyone in sight on their way to Amman, the Jordanian capital city. This prompted a call from the King of Jordan to Eric Jansen, asking for help. Eric was acutely aware that he must have been the last country the King called asking for help. He thought to himself before he replied that the King must be desperate with no one else offering aid. So, of course, he said he would help—would intervene— and that he could not tolerate a fanatical Islamist government run by a lunatic on their long border. Eric hung up the phone with the King with a creeping smile on his face. He had not anticipated the good fortune to actually be asked to intervene. He thought to himself, *What a public relations miracle!*

It took all his self-discipline to delay intervening—allowing the war to rage in neighboring Jordan. In the meantime, what Eric hoped would happen did happen. Hamas, the terrorist group ruling the Gaza strip, and Hezbollah, the terrorist proxy for Iran in Southern Lebanon, announced their solidarity with the new Syrian Islamist government by launching missiles at Israel. This was coupled with Palestinian riots in all major West bank cities. The only thing these different political groups had in common was their unified hatred of Israel and that they would do anything to destroy it. However, this common hatred of his country was what Eric was counting on to put his plan into action. Moreover, Eric felt confident that the Israel Defense Forces (IDF) was ready to defend the country against anything these groups could throw at it. Indeed, the rockets were launched en masse, hundreds from both Gaza in the South and Hezbollah in the North. This forced the air raid sirens to sound, sending the Israeli general population into air-raid shelters to protect themselves even though almost all the missiles were continuously shot down. Eric also knew that as soon as the enemy launched their missiles against Israel, the clock was ticking fast for him to unleash his new army.

But first Eric called a press conference with the Israeli High Command standing behind him. Just before the press conference started, he surprised his generals by telling them that Israel had developed a new weapon that consisted of robot soldiers using new handheld laser weapons supported by aerial battleships called Dragon Fire. He explained that the battleships would have even larger and stronger laser weapons and would be piloted by robots.

One of his generals said, "I'm glad you're telling us this. Otherwise, we might have shot one of them down."

"Let's not waste our missiles," Eric replied. "Because of the Dragon Fire's laser defenses, it is impossible to shoot them down. They use a new level of technology the world has never seen." When he said this, a hush fell over the Israeli High

Command. He added, "General Barak, put the IDF on full alert and close the borders between Jordan and us. But please make sure that any foreign diplomat from Jordan and their families are given asylum. However, no Jordanian citizen may enter per my order."

He then gave orders for the press conference to begin. He explained to the Israeli general public, now huddled in bomb shelters, what was about to happen. Standing on a small dais in a crowded room, with the Israeli High Command behind him and the press corp in front of him, Eric said, "I have an announcement to make about the missiles being fired at us again by our enemies. They are being fired in solidarity with the invasion of Jordan by the radical new government of Syria. At the request of the King of Jordan I have decided to intervene to help the Jordanians fight the radical Islamists. We have developed a new technology to do this that will be deployed for the first time. New soldier robots called Joshuas will be used for our defense fighting so that no Israeli soldier need engage the enemy. The beams of light you see lighting up the sky will be from our own aerial battleship laser weapons clearing the way for our robot soldiers. They will engage along all our borders. Remember, they represent a completely new technology developed by us. Because of this I don't expect it to be a long war. Our IDF soldiers will only be used as back up if necessary." It was a short press conference but earthshaking. It was given in Hebrew, not English, to minimize the announcement to the world community. However Eric knew that within an hour it would be translated into many different languages. No questions were allowed. What Eric didn't say at the press conference was that he expected IDF soldiers only to be needed to patrol newly conquered territory.

Two minutes later, by himself in a quiet corner of the corridor outside the press room, Eric called Elon Dagen and ordered him to deploy and institute the invasion plan on all borders. Elon hung up the phone and turned to the Captain 1 robot, saying, "Deploy and invade now! No prisoners!"

The Captain 1 robot replied, "By your command, Creator." Both Eric and Elon knew this was no retaliatory defense plan that Israel had employed so many times before. This was a full-scale invasion of its neighbors to end the cycle of attacks and counter attacks. They also knew that like Caesar crossing the Rubican River in Italy, they were casting the dye by crossing the Jordan River. This was a total life or death commitment!

The five Dragon Fire aerial battleships began the assault by delivering thousands of Joshua killer robots just inside all Israel's borders. It took almost an entire day to deploy several thousand robot Joshuas. By military standards this was very fast, given the incredible flying speeds of the aerial battleships coupled with how little space each robot took, packed like sardines inside the battleships. This allowed several hundred robot soldiers to be delivered with each trip. With the Joshua units in place at specific border sites, orders were uploaded to the control panels of the Dragon Fire battleships to commence the attack with one placed in orbit above the planet as back-up. Their laser beams methodically advanced scorching the ground and killing by incinerating everything they touched. Steady laser beams of death from above that were more than four miles (4.8km) wide moved along the earth, not only incinerating all living things it touched but also incinerating the concrete and steel of office buildings, hospitals, hotels and apartment houses in its path. General Dagen texted the Prime Minister that it seemed to him like mowing a lawn. It felt so easy!

These major laser blasts were followed on the ground by thousands of almost seven foot (2.1m) tall relentless killer robot soldiers that showed no mercy—for in order to show mercy you have to have emotions and morals which these machines lacked. They incinerated any humans who had not been in the direct path of the previous blasts. This included men, women, children and even pets—the entire human population was exterminated and turned to small clouds of black dust wafting on the winds.

The war was won so quickly and so thoroughly that the Israeli public, as they emerged from their bomb shelters, couldn't begin to comprehend the horror of what had actually happened. The secret robot production facility in the Negev with Brigadier General Elon Dagen in charge was turned into the command center for the war. This was done to keep it completely separate from the Israeli High Command military structure to avoid any interference.

At the beginning of the war, the population of the country of Jordan was estimated to be about 11.5 million people including about 2.5 million Palestinian refugees. After the war, the human population was zero. The population of the Gaza strip at the beginning of the war was almost 2 million people. After the war the human population was also zero. Before the war the population of southern Syria, south of Damascus to the Yarmuk River border was approximately 2 million people. After the war, with the exception of Israel's Druze allies totaling almost 200,000 people, the rest of the human population was reduced to zero. The same was true for southern Lebanon south of the Litani River. Its population was now zero except for a few Christian villages that had never allied themselves with Hezbollah, Israel's sworn enemy. Of course, the armies of both Jordan and Syria were completely annihilated. As for the riots in the West Bank which again centered in the Town of Jenin, Eric ordered his Dragon Fire battleships and killer robots to destroy the town as an example. Over 300,000 Palestinians who lived there were exterminated with laser blasts in a matter of hours.

What both Eric Jansen and Elon Dagen thought was good news about the full-scale genocide they had committed was that afterwards, there were no bodies to be buried. Hence, they thought there would be no smoking gun for any legal recourse. At least, that was what they hoped! Eric called Elon at the command center to heartily congratulate him on his quick victory. Elon's naturally gaunt looking face actually cracked a smile upon hearing this compliment. The incessant missile barrage attacks against Israel had been silenced forever. The victory also sent a strong and clear message to Israel's other enemies around the world, such as Iran, that Israel had the most advanced weapons on the planet and would use them. As planned, the Joshua robots patrolled Israel's new expanded borders while regular IDF soldiers patrolled the interior of the newly conquered lands. Whether the world realized it or not, a new age of warfare had just dawned on earth!

What followed surprised Eric. He had been very careful to let any diplomats of foreign countries posted to Amman to be allowed to cross the border. Many had used this escape route. But many diplomats along with many wealthy

Jordanians had also flown out of the country. He also kept a half an eye on world opinion. After recovering from the shock of what happened, almost every country in the world was outraged and condemned Israel and refused to acknowledge Israel's governance of any of its new territory. Eric had actually anticipated this reaction by developing an exceedingly close relationship with four foreign countries. He planned to circumvent any economic embargo by routing trade through them. In other words, although outwardly showing deep concern for world opinion, he actually didn't give a damn what most other countries thought or did. He also knew he had at his command a battle tested, victorious robot army. However, what took him by surprise was the Israeli public's reaction. He thought they would thank him for making them safer without spilling any Israeli blood. He got that totally wrong!

CHAPTER TWELVE

REVELATION

When the Israeli public emerged from three days of hiding in shelters from massive missile barrages, they soon realized how many millions of innocent people their Prime Minister had ordered murdered. The vast majority of the general public were horrified. Nevertheless, there were still some who supported his actions, mostly among the military and police. Within days there were massive demonstrations organized across the country against him demanding his resignation. His power base in the Knesset evaporated, too. It seemed that both religious Jews and secular Jews finally agreed on something—their current Prime Minister needed to resign. This kind of victory went against everything Judaism taught. The Attorney General of Israel started preparing documents to arrest him and charge him with genocide and treason.

Unfortunately for the country, Eric Jansen's growing mental psychosis made him less and less willing to compromise or tolerate different opinions. Although he did make an attempt to calm the situation. For example, he held several press conferences trying to justify what he had ordered by explaining that there would not be any more drugs or weapons smuggled into Israel through the Kingdom of Jordan. He also promised to return lands along the Jordan River to Israeli settlers. Lands that were given to the Kingdom of Jordan over the years as a gesture of goodwill to maintain the peace. He also stressed that Israel could build on the new lands, therefore lessening the housing shortage and bringing down real estate costs. But what he was actually thinking to himself as he made these announcements was that this conquest was so easy that his robot legions should conquer more territory and more countries. He was definitely not planning to give up any power or stop at Israel's new borders, especially since every week his robot production facility was producing more Joshua robot soldiers who were completely loyal to him!

In order to try to appease his critics, however, he allowed any Jordanians who wanted to return to their country the ability to do so. He would welcome them with open arms. Even as he announced this policy publicly, he couldn't help but expect treachery by any Jordanians who accepted this offer. His suspicions were confirmed when his Mossad spies informed him that under the pretext of civilians returning to their homeland, armed men boarded three 747 jet planes at the national airport in Tripoli, the capital of Libya. They had been financed by the government in exile of the former royal family of Jordan. Their destination was the newly reopened Amman International Airport. All the people on these flights were supposedly taking advantage of his offer to return. He alerted Captain 1, the command robot, to surround the planes with Joshua robots when they landed but make sure they hid themselves until the occupants disembarked. The airport workers who guided the planes to a stop and then brought the steps to the airplane doors for disembarking passengers were instructed to do so but then also run and hide. Eric decided to film everything to prove to the world that these soldiers, on orders from the remnants of the former monarchy, disembarked from the plane to attack Israel first. He also wanted the world to see the Joshua robots in action. He thought it would personally give him a stronger hand in any future negotiations he might have with anyone.

Each plane held 500 former Jordanian soldiers or paid mercenaries and their military equipment. After the planes landed, each plane quickly disembarked its soldiers who formed into battle formations to take control of the airport. As Eric and Elon watched the preparations for the attack via satellite video screen located in their robot command center, Eric turned to Elon saying, "They must have been well trained."

"Agreed," Elon responded.

Eric then said to Elon, "The moment the foot of one of these armed soldiers touched the ground I consider it an attack. Therefore, order Captain 1 robot to counterattack now but try to save the planes. They could be wired to explode."

Elon gave the order to the command robot who simply replied, "By your command Creator." Within minutes the Joshua robots burst forth with laser ray guns blazing from the airport control tower building and from the backs of two eighteen wheeler trucks parked on the side of the runway. The 1500 armed Jordanian soldiers were totally incinerated by the Joshua robot's laser weapons within minutes. The bullets they fired at the Joshuas just bounced off the robots. With lightning speed, the robots climbed the stairs and entered the planes. They incinerated all the pilots before any explosive devices could be detonated. Indeed, they found that all three planes had been wired to explode. This incident was viewed worldwide.

This incident also stripped Eric Jansen of any remaining patience he had to manage anybody he felt would or could oppose him. He quietly mused to himself, *Who needs patience when I have legions of killer robots at my command?* The overwhelming military advantage these battle tested robots displayed was obvious to him. Moreover, he now thought he had the excuse he needed to walk into the meeting of the full Knesset (Israeli Parliament), which had become a hot bed of opposition to him, with a hundred Joshua robots behind him. As he entered the meeting with his army in tow, he announced the following, "Based on the incident that just occurred at the Amman airport, I hereby rescind my offer of welcome to any former Jordanian citizens. I also annex all the land formally belonging to the former Kingdom of Jordan and open it up for Israeli settlement. The name of our new province west of the Jordan River will be Manasseh. I named it after one of our original twelve Hebrew tribes that was so large it had to settle on both sides of the river. I also formally annex and open the territory called the Gaza Strip for Israeli settlement. Also because of the continuous massive unrest in the country, most of it led by people in this room, I hereby dissolve the Knesset until further notice. I also order the house arrest of all members of Israeli Supreme Court and the Attorney General. All court activities will cease immediately until I personally make new appointments. All persons under house arrest will have robot security guards posted at their residences for their own safety." As he was announcing these changes to the government, the Joshua robots were encircling the outside of the room. The threat of bodily harm from the robots to the elected members of the Knesset was clear. His robot soldiers built to protect Israel from its neighbors had now become its prison guards!

The Knesset members were not stupid. They silently filed out of the room while they thought to themselves, *We will live to fight another day!* On this day, democracy died and the State of Israel became a dictatorship under the rule of a tyrant. Eric departed the Knesset building thinking to himself, *That was so easy. I really need to start planning my next successful war. Perhaps by taking the remainder of Syria and Lebanon as well as annihilating Iran? With another successful war, I'm sure the people will love me again.*

Eric's psychosis caused him to dramatically misread the mood and the moral character of the Jewish people which is and has always been, "To be a light unto the world." Eric's Joshua robots were spreading over the entire country, standing guard in plain site on major roads and intersections to keep order. The five Dragon Fire battleships were positioned in the sky above the country, low enough to be in plain sight to ostensively protect the country but also clearly to intimidate the population.

The High Command of the Israeli armed force's reaction to the Prime Minister's takeover of the government was mixed. Half of the members owed their promotion and position directly to him. The other half was willing to wait and see what unfolded, considering he had just tripled the size of the country without one Israeli death. The Shin Bet police were also happy to wait and see. Rioting and attacks on Israeli settlers in the West Bank had fallen to zero after he ordered his robots to exterminate the population of the Town of Jenin. This made the Shin Bet's job much easier. So, for the moment Eric had effectively neutralized any army or police opposition to his takeover of the government. However, inwardly they all had deep misgivings about how long it would take before the Prime Minister would have his robots start killing Israeli citizens who opposed him. Moreover, hatred of the killer Joshua robots and their new dictator was growing by the minute amongst the Israeli public who felt they had become prisoners of their robot guards in their own country. Nevertheless, General Barak, the head of the Israeli military High Command, still very much appreciated and understood Eric Jansen's determination to make his country stronger and more secure at any cost.

Mark had not seen or spoken to Eric for what seemed like an eternity. He had been following what was happening on the news. From what he could see, he was clearly worried about his partner. He called his old friends Jacob Kurtz and Sam Reichman who he knew were connected to Israeli intelligence. But all they could tell him beyond what he read or heard on the news was that Eric had surrounded himself with these killer robots, had taken over the government and was living in the PM's office. They confirmed the country was now a dictatorship. Both Jacob and Sam were also clearly worried about the future of the country and the mental state of their old friend Eric. They both knew about his previous PTSD episodes which they had helped to hide and which they now regretted. Mark even called Eric's mother and brother to see if they had heard anything. They had not heard anything either. Apparently Eric had cut himself off from all his old friends and family.

So, out of desperation and worry for his partner who he loved more than life itself, he found himself knocking on the door of the apartment of his friend and confidant Ari ben Halevi for advice. He was able to arrive alone without his security guard, Alisa, because he darted out of his house while she had gone on a quick shopping errand for him. What surprised Mark was how large the crowds had grown outside Ari's apartment. Once again the crowd parted to let him pass, which he found strange. Upon hearing a knock on his door, Ari immediately opened it, saying, "I am so glad to see you. I am amazed that the people in front of the place let you through. Not only are there hundreds of orthodox Jews but I have seen

Catholic priests and Protestant ministers now waiting outside, too. I even saw three Moslem mullahs yesterday. However, I think I am beginning to understand what's happening. Come on, I'll make us a cup of coffee and we can talk."

As they were sitting with their coffee, Mark blurted out that whenever he was with Ari he felt very calm and peaceful. But the reason for his visit this time was that he was extremely worried about Eric.

"Thank you," Ari replied. "I feel very comfortable around you, too. I have been following the news. And I have to tell you something you are not going to want to hear. I believe the abomination in God's message to me has to be the robots. And the Lord God is blaming Eric for their creation. That's what I think."

Mark needed a moment to process this. After a few minutes of silence between them, Mark said, "I see the truth that these robots are evil. But how do we fix this?" Mark was not yet ready to blame his partner for this robot horror engulfing the country.

Ari stared straight at Mark and said, "I haven't told anybody this, but I had another vision last night. God spoke to me saying that I must go to the top of the Temple Mount and blow His Trumpet. And the strangest thing is that you were in the vision, too, watching me. And now today you knock on my door. What a coincidence. How strange. But to tell you the truth, I am afraid to do it. After all, I am just a musician, a nobody."

Both men sat there in silence again, trying to make sense of what Ari just said. Mark spoke first. "Well then, if you think God told you to blow that damn trumpet on top of the Temple Mount, what are we sitting here for? Let's go do it. We can take my car." Mark continued, "By the way, what musical composition are you going to play up there?"

To which Ari responded, "Something new, something I heard in my dream last night. I hope you like it."

As Mark drove and Ari held the Holy Silver Trumpet, the dense crowds lining the streets all the way to the entrance to the Old City parted for their car. Mark noticed the crowds comprised all types of people: Jews, Christians and Moslems. All of the Abrahamic faiths were here, Mark thought to himself. Everyone was standing in silence as if waiting for something. He also noticed that many bowed their heads or averted their eyes as they passed, including the IDF soldier guards at the City entrance. This became very apparent as they walked along the streets of the Old City of Jerusalem toward the Temple Mount. Ari was carrying the Holy Silver Trumpet under his arm in plain sight for all to see. When they arrived at the Temple Mount, Ari chose to climb the stone staircase of the main entrance to the top and not use the wooden side entrance reserved for non-Moslems. Mark thought the Moslem guards would surely stop them, but all they did was bow their heads in silence as they passed. Mark thought that it must be the spiritual power of the Holy Silver Trumpet that Ari carried affecting so many people. Ari felt his heart start nervously beating faster as they approached the top of the Temple Mount. But he also made the decision to climb the stone steps in the exact middle of the stairs to the entrance. He noted to himself that the stone steps in the middle of the staircase entrance were original and not rebuilt or changed over the centuries. This somehow helped him feel more at ease as he walked on them. All this happened under the watchful eyes of the Joshua robots, who were now guarding everything in the country and would not tolerate any disturbances. Apparently the robots did not consider thousands of people silently watching and praying to God as any kind of a threat. Yet more and more robots, soon numbering in the thousands, were arriving by the minute to guard the ever increasing, enormously large crowds. They were not yet interfering with what was becoming crowds numbering in the hundreds of thousands. What no one noticed, except Elon Dagen, was that the order to send the robot army to surround the crowds came from the Captain 1 command robot who had defied his

Creator to issue it. It was the first time the Joshua command robot had disobeyed its Creator. This act of defiance terrified Elon and made him feel very vulnerable as he stood next to his seven foot (2.2m) creation in the Negev command center.

As Ari reached the top of the stone steps and entered the Temple Mount compound, he instinctively turned towards the Southwest corner. This is the corner closest to the current Jewish prayer plaza and just above the original City of David. When they arrived, Mark leaned over the waist-high stone wall surrounding it and said, "Wow, we're high. But what a view." Ari joined him to look.

"Don't you feel it?" Ari said. "The power of faith in God from the tens of thousands of people below praying. Its power is like a tidal wave crashing over the wall and covering us." Mark nodded in response that yes, he felt it too. It was after that comment that Mark noticed something change in his friend. In that moment, standing on the Holy Temple Mount like his ancestors before him, Ari finally found his faith in God. His new found faith centered him and gave him enormous spiritual strength.

"I'm not high enough," Ari said. "Let me stand on your shoulders to get on top of the building extension of the al-Aqsa Mosque. The building's corner is also the original corner of the Temple compound where the High Priests sounded the

Holy Trumpet. That's where I need to be." Mark felt scared for his friend to be on such flimsy footing at such a height. But nevertheless, Mark gave Ari a lift up, using his hands as a stirrup for Ari's foot. Mark steadied himself as Ari put a foot on his shoulder, giving Ari just enough lift to pull himself and the trumpet onto the roof.

Mark yelled to Ari, "Be careful where you walk! The stones up there may not be stable!" Up on the roof, Ari could feel his heart pounding while a feeling of exhilaration ran through his body.

Ari slowly walked to the corner of the Temple Mount, taking extreme care as he did so. He realized that Mark was correct—the stones on the edge of the Mosque's roof extension were narrower and definitely not as strongly built as the lower ones. As he carefully braced himself with each step, he couldn't help but notice what a beautiful sunny day it was to play his trumpet. The view of the city from the roof was unparalleled. He also couldn't help but notice the hundreds of thousands of people that were now praying below him. For the first time, he felt confident in himself that he was born to do what he was about to do. He softly said a prayer to God, saying, "Please God save your children from these abominations!" Then, as a hereditary descendent of God's consecrated High Priests, Ari put the Holy Silver Trumpet to his lips and began to blow. As he did this, all his insecurities melted away. The trumpet sounded, daring to call the Lord God Himself to war against these abominations. And the Lord God heard His High Priest and answered him. Almost immediately, Ari felt a quiver go through his body, further fortifying him. As the first note sounded, the sky began to darken. More and more swirling black storm clouds appeared directly above the Temple Mount. The swirling clouds expanded to cover the sky above the entire city and then the entire Holy Land, plunging every person and robot into midday darkness. Then came the powerful winds and rains—not gentle rains but drenching downpours—the kind that make it impossible to see your hand in front of your face. During the rain deafening thunderclaps began followed by lightning bolts. This was not lightning that any human alive had seen before. Lightning bolts the size of hundred story buildings rippled through black clouds high above, creating a spider webbed pattern in the sky. Monster lightning bolts this size had not been seen on earth since the days of the dinosaurs—a hundred million years ago. Pitch blackness followed by the bright whiteness of lightning punctuated the land. The bright Silver Trumpet shown like a beacon above the land against the whiteness of the lightning bolts. Through all this the people below were intensely praying to the Lord God. Strangely though, every one of them could clearly hear the sound of the Holy Trumpet above the thunderclaps and wind. Then, an even stranger event occurred. Every cellphone and every TV switched on, playing the music of the Holy Trumpet. What was stranger still was that afterwards everyone claimed they heard a different tune calling them to praise God. Some said they even heard HIS voice. The sound of His music enveloped the planet!

This huge storm covered every place where the manmade killer robots stood guard, drenching them with rainwater. The wind whipped the rainwater into every corner. The amount of electricity voltage in the air caused by these huge lightning bolts in the sky was record breaking. Even the people inside their homes who touched their walls got an electric shock. Peoples hair stood straight up. It is a scientific fact that water is an excellent conductor of electricity. So what happened when the robots drenched with rain came into contact with the highly charged electricity in the air? After a few minutes, the atmospheric electrical voltage covering the wet metal limbs and skulls of the robots disrupted the delicate liquid in the robot brains by overloading and overheating it. Finally, the electrical impulses that controlled the robot brain shut down—ceased to function! Or, in other words, they were electrocuted where they stood! As their brains ceased to function the robot bodies became stiff and unbalanced, falling over like a heap of metal junk.

The Dragon Fire aerial battleships patrolling the airspace above the Holy Land were also destroyed. The storm developed so quickly that they were unable to rise above it in time. The rain thoroughly coated the outside of the battleships while the high voltage electrical charges generated from multiple lightning strikes enveloped them. It gradually destabilized their laser defense shields and antigravity fusion engines. However, instead of crashing to earth, the unstable power of the fusion engine spun three of them with their robot crews into the sun; made one crash and explode on the surface of the moon; and spun the last one into an asteroid belt between Mars and Jupiter, tearing it apart.

Through their cellphones and satellite broadcasts, almost everyone in the world saw what happened. This included Eric Jansen, barricaded in the Prime Minister's office complex, and the genius scientist Elon Dagen, working four floors below in the robot production and command facility. While watching the destruction of his robot army on the large TV in the command center, Elon was now certain that the Captain I command robot standing next to him had become sentient by the way the robot was emotionally reacting to the destruction of his fellow robots. Finally, the Joshua command robot looked directly at Elon and said, "This destruction of my fellow robots is your fault. We do not wish the humans any harm." Elon knew this meant that by thinking for himself, it wouldn't be long before the command robot would no longer follow any orders and would probably turn on him. Elon was terrified, as this was happening much sooner than he had planned. Thus, his survival instinct kicked in. So, while the Captain 1 command robot was still focused on the destruction of his fellow robots, he quickly walked, almost running, to his office. He locked himself in there trying to protect himself against a robot attack. However, less than five minutes later, the production facility took a direct hit from two monster lightning bolts which destroyed everything and everyone, except for Elon Dagen who luckily remained secure in his fortified office. In this case, it was true that lightning did strike twice in the same place!

Ari kept blowing the Holy Trumpet for about thirty minutes. Blowing a trumpet on top of the Temple Mount in the brutal wind and rain was very tiring even for a strong, young guy like him. He felt the wind swept rain stinging his hands and face. His lips and hands ached. But his faith in God gave him the strength to continue. Strangely, he knew when to stop playing and that he had played long enough to destroy all the robot abominations. Not one robot escaped God's wrath.

He deeply felt that he had followed what God instructed and that the Lord God was pleased. As soon as the sound of the Holy Trumpet stopped, the storms stopped. The sky cleared and the sun began to shine again. The only thing noticeably different was that the air smelled clean, even sweet, while a gentle wind caressed his face. The next big endeavor on his schedule was getting down from this very precarious perch. As he turned to step away from the corner, the still wet, slippery stones caused him to lose his balance for just a moment. He recovered immediately but not before he accidentally let go of the Holy Silver Trumpet. It went crashing down the outer wall of the Temple Mount, hitting the stone floor more than seventy feet (21.3m) below. However, this time when he let go of the trumpet, it changed back into the condition he found it in – that of a relic that was thousands of years old. Losing its silvery shine, it turned back into a brittle, deeply corroded, delicate piece of brown metal. Its transformation occurred the moment it left Ari's hand.

So, what happened when a delicate piece of ancient metal drops and hits a hard stone floor 70 feet (21.3m) below? It literally shattered, turning to powder that was scattered all over by an unexpected gust of wind. Mark saw what happened and immediately yelled to Ari, "Forget it. Concentrate on yourself. Don't look down. Look at me." Ari swallowed hard to calm himself. He then proceeded to slowly lower himself off the roof, finally hanging by his hands. Mark again yelled to Ari, "Let yourself go. I am underneath you. Trust me. I will break your fall." With that Ari let himself drop, falling on Mark. The next thing Mark said was, "Boy, you're heavy! Get off me!" Ari immediately got up and offered Mark his hand to help Mark up too. Then, they both walked to the waist high wall on the edge of the Temple Mount and looked over its side to see what happened. They were sorry to see that the Holy Trumpet was destroyed, but agreed it had served its purpose and was now truly lost forever. They also noticed that the huge crowds had begun to disperse and that the robot guards around the periphery of the crowds were lying stiff and lifeless on the ground. They agreed to leave the Temple Mount as soon as possible since Mark was very impatient to find his partner, Eric.

First, Mark drove Ari back to his apartment in Tel Aviv. On the way back, Ari confessed to Mark that after much thought, he had decided to become a rabbi. After what had just happened he sensed, or rather hoped, that there would be a rebirth of faith in God around the world. Mark smiled, noticing that something had changed in his young friend. Ari had become more mature and confident in himself. Mark told him that he thought Ari would make a great rabbi. But now Mark knew he must find Eric. As Ari got out of Mark's car, he turned to his friend and said, "Again, Thank you for your help. Couldn't have done this without you. So, goodbye, until we meet again in the next life!"

"You know, you and your metaphysical sensitivity can be creepy sometimes," Mark responded.

"Ok," Ari said. "Then how about lunch next Tuesday? You're buying."

Mark retorted, "That's better. It's a date." As they parted and Mark drove off to find Eric, Ari couldn't shake his premonition that he would not see his friend Mark again. He hoped he was wrong.

Elon Dagen managed to leave his office, lock it and crawl up the side of the hole in the ground where his production and command center used to be. Surveying the area, he was aghast at the destruction. He immediately texted Eric Jansen that the production facility and command center had been destroyed but that he was alive and that his office where the records and files for the robot and aerial battleship projects were kept was still intact. He also said in the text that he had figured out what went wrong. He had protected the robots from grounding with rubber soles on their feet but had not protected them from electrical overload. He thought this would be an easy fix but wanted to do an autopsy on one of the Joshua robots first. Because he still had his notes in his office, he thought he could have the robot army up and running again in less than two years. What he did not put in the text was his fear that the Joshua command robot had become sentient and thus uncontrollable. He thought he needed to discuss that with Eric face to face. Just after he sent his text, he thought he heard an explosion behind him and sound of rushing water. The production facility had been built on the edge of an ancient wadi. A wadi is the Middle Eastern term for a ravine or gully. This wadi had been dry for many thousands of years. But when it rains hard—very hard like just recently—wadis flood, turning into murderous rivers of fast moving rock, trees and mud. When he turned to see what the explosion was, before he could blink, he was hit with a wall of water, mud, stone and debris with the speed of a freight train that buried him and his records room under tons of mud. The mud that buried him and the records room very quickly dried to the consistency of concrete when the hot desert sun hit it, while the desert sand was already blowing over it hiding everything. Nevertheless, the records room survived intact!

Mark was beside himself with worry about Eric. He called everyone he knew to try and find him. Eric wasn't answering his phone. After the fall of the robot army, the Knesset members poured back into the parliament chamber. In less than an hour they passed a bill impeaching the Prime Minister. The current President of the Knesset, Saul Jacoby, became the acting PM. The newly freed Israeli Attorney General issued an arrest order accusing Eric Jansen of genocide and treason. The newspapers and the global press was full of the news. They also carried a story about the disappearance and probable death of Brigadier General Elon Dagen. The Supreme Court cleared its schedule for Eric's trial. The Attorney General was asking for the death penalty!

Finally Mark received a call from Eric asking him to meet him at their house. Mark frantically drove there. He walked into their house and found Eric sitting on the sofa in the living room. But he didn't look like the man Mark knew. His clothes were dirty. His hair was disheveled. He hadn't shaved or bathed in days. And it looked like he hadn't slept, either. Mark immediately realized that there was something very wrong with his partner. This opinion was further confirmed when he saw a pistol lying on Eric's lap. Eric's eyes were that of wild man just staring into space. As Mark approached him, Eric slowly turned his head and said, "Oh, It's you. I was wondering where you were. Why did you betray me like everyone else?"

Mark responded with as much gentleness in his voice as he could muster, "What are you talking about?"

Eric's eyes started to focus on Mark, as he said, "I saw you up there on the Temple Mount. You sided with your friend against me."

Hearing the craziness in Eric's voice and the look in his eyes, Mark knew Eric wasn't thinking right. He was afraid Eric would hurt himself with that pistol. He had no fear for himself, however. "Come, let me give you a hug," Mark said, "I know you need a hug."

He really did think they needed to hug each other. But Mark's other reason for getting close was that he thought he could gently get the pistol away from his partner. Mark sat down on the sofa next to Eric and embraced him. While embracing him, Mark reached for the pistol on Eric's lap. But Eric was a former Special Forces and Mossad agent well trained in handling weapons and subterfuge. He simply grabbed the gun first while looking straight into Mark's eyes and said, "I love you. But I know what they say about me and I'm no traitor." With that Eric aimed the pistol diagonally under his chin to kill himself. What surprised Eric, making him hesitate for a moment, was that Mark grabbed the pistol at the same time to alter its aim. Eric accidentally fired one bullet into the ceiling. Both men knew that Eric was much stronger and better equipped for such a struggle. Yet, in this moment, Eric had what can only be explained as an out of body experience. He saw himself looking down on Mark struggling to get control of his pistol, fighting to save Eric's own life with more ferocity than he had ever seen Mark display. When he saw this something deep inside him changed. Something that made him reconsider what the heck he was planning on doing to himself. Perhaps it was him recognizing that Mark still loved him enough to fight for him. Or perhaps it was the sound of the gun shot that helped him snap out to it. Whatever caused it didn't matter. What mattered was that his emotional balance and sense of self returned while his black side went back into its locked box. In other words, he became himself again.

Before Eric had time to react to his new state of mind, everything changed. Hearing the gun shot, Alisa Reichman followed by a squad of Israeli Special Forces burst through their front door. Alisa took one look at the two men struggling for a gun and took action. It wasn't her first time at a gun fight! What happened next was the reason her nickname within the Mossad was the Viper. At lightning speed like a viper's strike, she used the top of a living room chair as a brace to pole-vault over it, kicking both men in the head with the bottom of her shoes as she landed. This whole time, she never took her eyes off the pistol. Because of the strength of the impact of her kick and her entire body landing on them a moment later, she was able to twist the pistol free from their hands. The Special Forces soldiers tackled and subdued Eric and Mark immediately afterwards.

Arriving just behind the Special Forces soldiers was General Barak, Chief of the Israeli High Command. He didn't bother introducing himself. He just said, "There will be no trial for you Mr. former Prime Minister. You still have friends in this country. Our acting Prime Minister, Saul Jacoby, has negotiated a deal with the Attorney General for you to leave the country. You both will be put on a plane tonight and go into exile. Eric Jansen, you are hereby banished. You can never return. There are four countries that have volunteered to give you sanctuary. You can let the pilot know which one you pick when you are airborne. There is no time to pack. We all must leave in secret immediately to the military airbase where your plane is waiting. The public will not be informed for 24 hours. No matter which country you pick, a house and security will be provided. The alternative is life in prison or execution. So I advise you to take the deal. I'm here personally to make sure this goes smoothly."

Both Mark and Eric were stunned at this new situation but took the offer. As they left their beautiful home which Mark dearly loved, he realized it was for the best. As he walked past Alisa while rubbing the side of his still throbbing head where her shoe hit, he said, "You have a kick like a mule. But I guess it could have been worse. You could have been wearing spiked high heels instead of flats!"

This elicited a chuckle from her. All she said was, "I'll miss you both."

Mark responded, "Tell everyone goodbye for us." She gave him a quick hug and nodded that she would.

They were being led out of their house separately, with Eric exiting first. Looking ahead of him, Mark recognized the soldiers surrounding Eric. They were the ones from Eric's former Special Forces unit! He overheard one of them call Eric, "Professor" which was the nickname his old comrades in the army called him. He then saw Eric laugh and turn around to wink at him. Mark could tell that Eric had returned to his old self, but that they would have to prepare for a new and uncertain future. In the car on the way to the airport, Mark said a silent prayer thanking God that they were still alive, together, and that the political part of their lives was finished. As they were sitting side by side in the back seat of a car being driven to a military airport, Mark turned to look at his partner and sensed Eric was deeply engrossed in thought. But Mark couldn't tell what he was thinking about. As Eric's thoughts were clearing, he was realizing that he was the only one still alive who knew the location of the robot production facility where, according to Elon Dagen's last text to him, Elon's office was still intact. An office containing records and files that could be used to raise another robot army. And didn't Elon's last text also say it could be done in less than two years? A small, tight smile crossed his lips as he processed this thought.

AUTHOR'S NOTE

Thank you for reading my book. I hope you enjoyed it. Please write a review on the sales platform of your choice.
Mark Akst, author

ABOUT THE AUTHOR

Mark Akst is retired and lives in Fort Lauderdale, Florida. His fourth novel, *The Joshua Abomination*, is an interconnected but standalone novel that follows the exploits of his characters from previous books. His passionate hobbies are Biblical archeology and Middle East history and politics. He holds a Bachelor of Arts degree from the University of Pennsylvania and a MBA from New York University. He is retired from the hospitality business and has traveled extensively through North America, Europe and the Middle East. All his novels are written for his readers as a fun escape in a stressful world. You can contact him on his website at:

https://markakst.com

**Previous Novels
By Mark Akst**

·⚬ঝ⚬·

The Mark Cohn Series
King Herod's Treasure
The Secrets of the Saffron Mountain
The Mossad Warrior Spy